*Upon This Mountain*

# Upon This Mountain

*Timothy Wangusa*

*Black Star Books and Head of Zeus would like to thank the following organisations: The Miles Morland Foundation, The Ford Foundation, and Africa No Filter. This publication was made possible through their support.*

First published in the Heinemann African Writers Series in 1989
by Heinemann Educational Publishers

This edition published in 2024 by Black Star Books and Head of Zeus,
part of Bloomsbury Publishing Plc.

9 7 5 3 1 2 4 6 8

A catalogue record for this book is available from the British Library.

ISBN (PB): 9781035900886
ISBN (E): 9781803288819

Typeset by Siliconchips Services Ltd UK

Printed and bound by CPI Group (UK) Ltd,
Croydon, CR0 4YY

Head of Zeus Ltd
First Floor East
5–8 Hardwick Street
London ECIR 4RG

WWW.HEADOFZEUS.COM

To the memory of DEBORAH my wife
Who only saw half of it

*Chapter One*

Many, many millet granaries ago, he was mother's child, and she was the child's mother. And they sat in the shade on the verandah of the main house: mother with her legs stretched in front of her, to let the midday meal sink into her bones; and he fast asleep beside mother, with his head in mother's lap.

And there before them was the exalted, everlasting mountain, covered in a dull haze and buoying up the horizon in the far distance. For as far as the eye could see in the opposite direction the strong after-harvest sun had dried and browned the land, and in the near distance a wavy line of bush fire was creeping and advancing along the brow of a hill.

Then suddenly the noise of galloping cattle with tinkling neck-bells and the herdsboy song-shouting and galloping with the cattle towards the perennial Manafwa River. And the bells' tinkling *nklo nkling nklo nkling nklo nkling* rudely woke Mwambu.

And he opened his eyes upon his mother: mother's face, mother's arms, mother's lap. Tendermost mother as before. And he felt the itch inside him to suck at the breast. To clamber into her cosy, eversure lap and suck.

'Mother mine,' he said, rising and clambering. But as he reached out for the breast, he tripped over her legs and fell against her womb. And then came the rebuff.

'*Pthwoh!*' she spat into his face and pushed him away in visible anger. 'You a man!' His face went into a shocked, wide-mouthed, closed-eyed, noiseless contortion… 'You such a grown-up…!'

*Mother-bad-good-bad-good-why?*

'… To go harassing me for my breast as if it was yours! And after you've just eaten so much food!'

And now the noiseless contortion broke into a shrill, loud and long cry of anguished bafflement.

'And falling against my stomach like that! Do you know what's inside it?' He did not know that his little sister Khalayi was someday to come out of it.

Everything reeled before him. Reeling millet granary. Reeling world. Trembling skyline through the teardrops. Mountain falling into the valleys and valleys falling onto mountain. The way they had appeared to do some time back when he had bent over and looked at the world from between his legs and he had shuddered and quickly stood up and shaken his head.

'And stop crying at once! Or I'll beat you and then you can cry properly. Do you hear?' And so saying, she pulled him to herself, threw him upon her lap with his face downward and smacked his buttocks. *Pah pah pah!* He cried the more, stamping the ground with his little naked feet, and mixing mucus with tears.

'I said stop crying!' She raised her hand in apparent preparation for a fresh onslaught. 'Mwambu, stop crying or I'll...'

But a very powerful voice saved him.

'Who is that beating Mwambu?' His father's voice! From the house. A strong and concerned voice.

'What has Mwambu eaten? Eh! Come this way, Mwambu. Come to me in the house.'

And instantly his toddling feet were fleeing from mother's presence to father's voice, through the instinctively remembered door. Before him was an outstretched arm. And now both arms. And then he found himself lifted by strong arms and placed on a strong soft bed. His father held him close to his breast and said:

'And now do not cry any more,

You are a man...

Do not cry, mother is bad...

I will beat her for you

(You out there, what did Mwambu eat?)

Now do not cry any more...

Let me wipe your tears,

Then you can sleep...

Here beside me on the bed:

That is right, do not cry,

You are a man...'

Some days later Mayuba, the newly married wife of his

cousin Kuloba, came into the courtyard and threw him a challenge:

'How are you, husband of mine?' she asked. 'I hear that you're no longer sucking mother's breast. You've done a very good thing. And it shows how very wise you are! You've seen that you're now a big man. And that's the truth. And on my part, I am myself now completely ready to be your wife. Tell me, aren't you happy? I'm happy myself… Come, let's go to our house. Tonight you must share my bed with me. Come at once and let's go to our house… Come let's go, I say. I am your wife. Your brother has gone on a journey today and I have no husband. You must come and keep his place in the bed warm… Hey, are you running away? What are you afraid of? Poor me, what a husband…!'

In the evening of the following day he went with his mother to the fountain, carrying a miniature saucepan. They went downhill all the way. And the mountain was piercingly beautiful with the soft, golden light of the setting sun upon its rock face. Then they climbed steeply down into the trough of the fountain and he was so sorry he could not see the sun-draped mountain from there.

There were so many women drawing water. Drawing water and filling their pots and pans and talking loudly and laughing, laughing. Oh so many of them. Little girls. Big girls. Grown-up women with bulging breasts. Very old women with loose, withered breasts pointing downwards.

Drawing water at sunset. Filling their pots and pans and laughing.

His mother greeted them, 'Peace to you all, women of the fountain.'

And they all replied, 'Peace to you, late-comer to the fountain.' And Wopuwa's old wife carried on the greeting.

'What news from this wide world, Masaaba's own?' she asked, and Mwambu wondered how his mother was owned by his father.

'No news,' answered his mother. 'What news from your end of it?'

'No news,' returned Wopuwa's old wife. And then she removed her pipe from her toothless mouth and spat on the grass beside her to clear her mouth.

'You say no news,' she remarked, raising her eyebrows. Then looking sideways like a chameleon at Mwambu, she asked, 'But what is this I hear about someone on this earth who never wanted to stop sucking his mother's breast?' All the women burst out laughing:

'Aheheheheheheh-----e!
Wuwu!
Aeee-----e!
Mayi mukhasi weye!'

[My mother woman O!]

Some of the women clutched their pots as support and

others pressed upon their ribs, pretending that they had been so amused that their sides were aching.

Holding on to his mother's loincloth, Mwambu kept his eyes on the ground and twisted his right toe in the mud by the water's edge, his back turned to the painful women.

But to his further discomfort, a woman with pointed breasts who had stripped down to the waist and was bending forward and washing her upper half in the running water, now added, 'But what I would like to know is, did he mean to go on sucking the breast till he had grown a beard?'

*'Ahehehehehehehehehehehe------e!*
*Wuwu!*
*Aeee-----e!*
Mayi mukhasi weye!'

Mwambu choked with shame and anger and worked away more furiously at the mud with his toe. Then mercifully his mother rallied: 'But who says that he had been suckled for too long? As soon as he knew that he should not feed on the breast any more, he simply stopped.'

'Yes, yes,' pursued the half-naked woman. She was now squatting in the water and washing her lower half with a deliberately loud noise of her open hand upon the water, her loincloth held above her knees. 'Yes, Masaaba's own. But had he refused to grow up, all these girls you see here would have rejected him. They would have shrugged their shoulders and said, "Who can love a mother's spoiled child?"'

*'Ahehehehehehe-----e!'*

Choking! Oh he was choking with wordless anger. And then once more his mother came to the rescue, and this time conclusively.

'Let's be going, Mwambu. These women never run short of ugly things to say. Here's your saucepan of water.' She put the miniature saucepan on his head. 'Good! That's a useful man. Stay well and sleep well, all you gossiping women.'

They climbed out of the trough of the fountain. And gradually, to his unspeakable relief, the voices of the women died behind him. But when he looked to see the sun, it had already sunk behind the hill beyond his father's house, and the golden light had faded from the face of the mountain.

Just below the fountain there was a dark and fearsome grove. Children did not play near it. It was Mukimba's grove. Mukimba was Kangala's father, and Kangala became Mwambu's friend. But Kangala was much taller and older than Mwambu.

Mukimba was a strange man. He was very tall and as black as the soot on a cooking pot. His eyes were red like those of a cock. When there was no rain and the crops started turning brown, Mukimba would go into his grove and make the rain fall. And when there was too much rain and the weeds were growing faster than the crops, Mukimba would go into his grove and the rain would stop. All the grown-up people respected him very much and called him *Umutikityekulu*, he who tickles the heavens. If you did not behave well in his presence he could tickle the sky and lightning would eat you up before you could wink again! And they said he could make the foreskin grow again on a freshly circumcised youth who said dirty things within his hearing!

Kangala and Mwambu ran breathlessly toward their target. It was a huge tree. It was Kangala's school. They called it a subgrade school. And on Sunday the tree also became the house of God. They were running to beat the drum because the teacher had told Kangala that God was going to be born as a person-baby under that tree in a few days' time. And Kangala had told Mwambu.

They got to the tree at the same time as three other boys. Kangala took down the drum from the tree-church. Then they took up sticks. Kangala positioned himself at the larger end, and Mwambu at the smaller end of the drum, and they started to beat it. Mwambu was very thrilled by the sound they produced on the drum.

Two of the other boys asked to have their turn. And in what harmony they beat it! At first a few and distinct strokes, then quick ones that ran into each other with rising tempo, worked into a rhythm of happy announcement. They beat it loudly, they beat it softly, they beat it furiously, they beat it steadily, they beat it rapidly. And it boomed and throbbed and rolled.

Then, on God's birthday, a man in a white *kanzu* walked to the front, through the crowd seated under the tree. But to Mwambu's disappointment, the man was not carrying the baby-God. But he said that God had actually been born. That happy morning. Only that he could not be seen. He was with them right under that tree. That happy morning. Baby born to be God. And his name was Owner of Peace, Giver of Joy, Leader of Men. That happy morning. And whoever had that baby boy God as his friend would never die! Whoever did not become his friend was dead already!

Mwambu marvelled at the so many walking-but-dead people. All dead because they were not friends with the baby-God. As for himself, he would be the best friend of the baby-God. In fact, he and the baby-God immediately became such close friends that in his wonderment Mwambu also became a baby-God. And he told old men and old women such wonderful things. And all the men and women and little boys and little girls applauded him so much that wings sprouted on his shoulders and he flew upwards and hovered above the admiring crowd. They applauded without end and he danced to their song of him without tiring, without...

'And so,' concluded the man in the white *kanzu*, 'as you feast in your homes today, remember...'

'Oh... baby-God!' silently added Mwambu. 'Baby-God. Baby-God and the drums!'

## Chapter Two

Khalayi had been born beautiful and healthy. With the passing seasons she grew from a baby to a little girl and started speaking human words and eating adult food. After the evening meal she and Mwambu would carefully store away the left-over food behind the water-pot. At night the ancestors came and ate the steam from the food and in the morning Khalayi and Mwambu ate the remainder.

After eating the evening meal one night, the family lay awake talking. And Mwambu said,

'Tell us a story, our mother. A good story with giants in it.'

'Yes,' joined in Khalayi. 'Tell us a story, our mother. Like that one of yesterday.'

And so their mother turned on her side and told them one of her favourite stories.

'Long, long ago there was a young man called Mwambu, and he had a sister called Sera. Now Sera was very beautiful, and brown like *induli* fruit. Many young men from the mountain and from the plains heard of her beauty and came to woo her.

'The first one to come was a tall and handsome herdsman from the plains. He arrived early in the morning and sat on the crossbar of the millet granary as a sign of what he had come for. Mwambu saw him and greeted him. He told his father about him and he came out of the house and also greeted him and asked him the reason for his early morning visit. "Old one," replied he, "I have a hoe without a handle and I have come looking for one in your courtyard." "Do you mean to say," returned Mwambu's father, pretending to be surprised, "that you have spied a useless handle in this homestead, young man?" And the visitor replied humbly, "Old one, if it'll not annoy you, my answer is Yes." In the end Sera was told about the suitor, but she shrugged her shoulders and said that she did not like him. And her reason was that she was waiting for the most handsome suitor and that he was yet to come.

'One after another countless suitors came, and one after another they were all rejected. And Sera's reason was always the same. She was waiting for one who was yet to come.

'Then one day there came a suitor who was more handsome than any of the young men that had ever been seen in the land. He had the body of a warrior, teeth so white as if he never ate on them, and a winsome voice like a well-tuned *litungu*. He too stated the purpose of his visit and he too was duly rejected by Sera.

'But when he rose to go away he said to Sera in a most

luring voice, "O you beautiful one, brown like *induli* fruit, won't you see me off even the distance of a stone's throw?" To the surprise of everyone, Sera complied and walked with her suitor for a short distance. But at the end of that distance, the handsome suitor said, "O you beautiful one, brown like *induli* fruit, if only I could walk with you for another stone's throw!" Again, Sera granted him his request. But at the end of that distance, too, the handsome suitor begged for the same favour. He kept on renewing the request many times; and every time Sera enchanted by his voice granted him his wish. At last they reached a far-away land, farther than from here to the farthest lake. Then suddenly the handsome suitor stopped, turned round to Sera and said, "You that are so beautiful and proud – now look at me!" And so saying, he threw off his human mask and when Sera looked to see her suitor – behold, it was Wanesirikhe the Monster.

'Sera threw up her arms in great terror, screaming and shouting. And in her despair, she cried in song:

*'Wo papa Mwantsa*
*Wo yaya Mwambu*
*Kusolo kwamakana kwandya*

[Oh father Mwantsa
Oh brother Mwambu
I am eaten by the terrible
                    Monster]

'Now Sera's voice was sharper than any bell that has ever dangled from the neck of a cow. And that day Mwambu had taken his father's cattle beyond seven hills and across the wilderness in search of green pasture. When he heard Sera's voice he said, "That's my sister I hear crying!" And picking up his spear and panga and shield and calling upon his dogs to follow him, he sped across the wilderness as no other man has ever run, nor ever will. And in less time than it takes dust to absorb saliva, he arrived in the far-away land and stood face to face with Wanesirikhe. But his sister was nowhere to be seen.

'Then Wanesirikhe looked with scorn upon Mwambu and asked him, "Are you brother or lover of her that used to be alive?" "I'm her fearless brother, you heap of an idiot!" replied Mwambu. "Will you set her before my eyes at once?"

'Hearing these surprisingly bold words from a tiny human being, Wanesirikhe burst out laughing. And his laughter was like the noise of thunder or the sound of a mighty river tumbling down a steep mountainside, and his giant mouth was redder than a blacksmith's forge.

'"She's," said Wanesirikhe, pointing to his bulging paunch, "she's in here, in my…"

'"And *there* is for your boasting large mouth!" said Mwambu, sinking his spear into Wanesirikhe's belly. "And *there!* And *there!* And *there!*"

'Suddenly panic and terror seized Wanesirikhe. He grew wild, roaring with the acute pain of the spear-thrusts as he tried to lay his hands on Mwambu. But Mwambu was too quick for him, jumping this way and that way and covering himself with his shield and spearing Wanesirikhe in several places. Streams of blood were by now running out of Wanesirikhe's smitten body and soaking and reddening the desert sand. After a short while Wanesirikhe could not move at all. He swayed on the spot, heaving with difficulty. Then staggering towards Mwambu, he slumped down in a gigantic heap, dead!'

'*Wowe!*' cried Mwambu and Khalayi.

'Quickly Mwambu split open Wanesirikhe's belly with his panga. But Sera was not there. She had been completely eaten up, and all that remained of her was her navel. Now while the dogs feasted on Wanesirikhe's entrails, Mwambu took Sera's navel and running and finding *lufufu*, that mystical herb, he rubbed it round the navel, and behold, out of the navel – up sprang Sera, whole and alive again!'

'*Ayaya!*' cried Mwambu and Khalayi in peak excitement.

'And thus,' continued their mother, 'Mwambu defeated Wanesirikhe the Monster and brought back his sister from the dead. And thus Sera learnt that it is bad to be beautiful and proud.

'My story has ended there,' concluded their mother. '*Pthwoh!* Story, may you remain a dwarf while I grow,' said she.

'*Pthwoh!* Story, may you remain a dwarf while I grow,' said Mwambu.

'*Pthwoh!* Story, may you remain a dwarf while I grow,' said Khalayi.

'*Pthwoh!* Story, may you remain a dwarf while I grow,' said their father.

During his mother's retelling, Mwambu had got right inside the story and become the story. After the end he still remained inside it, and from there he now ventured out to ask, 'But, mother, when I had killed Wanesirikhe…'

'Now, now!' interrupted his father. 'How many Mwambus are there in this world? Shall we not sleep tonight because of questions? Next year I had better send you to school. To Namwombe Primary School where, they say, they ask and answer all questions in broad daylight. And not here, where eyes are heavy with sleep.'

*Chapter Three*

Masaaba and Mwambu set out just as the sun was beginning to peep above the mountain. Peeping and quivering like the young of a cow when it first looks on the world.

Wearing an old pair of short trousers of his father's and a *suka* that left his shoulders bare, Mwambu ran through the wet grass at the heels of his father. With a raised stick, Masaaba kept on beating the dew off the grass in their way, so that father and son went along without being soaked, while the taller grass, swaying back into the path, made an exit archway for the short Mwambu.

His mother, holding Khalayi by the hand, stood outside the house mumbling words of good luck upon the two sojourners. She followed them with anxious eyes till they turned the bend and entered the field of *matooke*. And just as they disappeared from view, the full sun showed above the mountain.

'Father,' called Mwambu as they emerged from the field of *matooke*, all agog with a sense of adventure. 'Father, shall we reach the top of the mountain?'

'Oh, no,' replied Masaaba. 'We shall not go that far.'

'Is the school not on the mountain?'

'No. It is just two hills away.'

Oh, then they would not reach the end of the world that day! regretted Mwambu. If only the school had been on top of the mountain. Where the earth touched heaven and where the world ended. And how was it that heaven and earth met very far away from their home in all directions? He had often wondered. Was there an unseen pillar in his village holding up heaven at the centre? Like the middle pillar of a house.

'Father,' he resumed the subject, skipping behind Masaaba, 'have you ever touched heaven?'

'No. That's a strange question. No one has ever touched heaven.'

'No one?' He was so surprised that no one had. 'But you have climbed the mountain?'

'Yes. To pull up young bamboo shoots. But that was a long time ago. When I was a youth, just a little older than you. It took us a whole day. No, three days, getting there and back. We nearly froze to death up there at night.'

'Then you have been on top of the mountain.'

'No. Bamboos do not grow on top of the mountain.'

'Where do they grow?'

'On the slopes. The lower slopes. Above the bamboo forest, trees do not grow. Only grass and mountain myrtle and mountain fern. All the way to the peak. And I have never been to the peak, as there is nothing to get from there.'

Oh, what a pity! thought Mwambu. How could he not have wanted to get to the peak?

'But what is there above the peak?' pursued Mwambu.

'I told you there is nothing. Just clouds. Clouds and nothing.'

The words stuck and echoed in Mwambu's mind. Just clouds. Clouds and nothing. Clouds and nothing. Clouds and nothing… And his father had never wanted to climb to the peak of the world. And so he had never…

His thoughts were interrupted by a stream that suddenly sprang into their view. A stream of clean and fresh water that gently gurgled among the stones on its way down, down, down… to where? wondered Mwambu. He followed the stream in his mind till very, very far away at the world's end, he started falling down a steep cliff and his mind took fright and sped back to his body walking behind his father.

They stopped on a large stone in the middle of the stream and Masaaba said he was going to wash Mwambu's legs for him. Supporting himself on his father's shoulder, Mwambu put his right foot forward, and then his left. He looked down at the strong muscles of his father's arms and his rich matted beard as he squatted below him on the stone and an overwhelming, momentary feeling swept through him and he longed to grow up and look like him.

'There!' said Masaaba. 'You're now clean enough to read in books and talk *fotifoti*. Those three buildings you see over there are Namwombe Primary School. I'll take you to the headmaster first. You'll have to walk back home on your own in the afternoon. From today you're a big man.'

At break time, the tough boys converged upon the grass by the sunrise end of the main classroom block, and Kunikina the Tortoise led the assault on Mwambu.

'I say,' called Tortoise, so nicknamed because of the marks scabies had imprinted upon his skin once upon a time. 'I say, you people, have you seen the newest green leaf?'

'Yes, man,' replied Wayero the Terrible, who had repeated Primary One twice already. 'He was put in my stream, and do you know what? He can't read even the first line of the alphabet! I will show him how not to be so green.'

'Is he not that one shying away behind the eucalyptus tree?' put in Kongo the Double-Eater of insatiable appetite.

'Hey, you *mpioko*,' shouted the Terrible One. 'Come running here! Did you hear? Okay, double quick!'

Mwambu wonderingly, fearfully walked over. Within seconds the boys had formed a ring round him.

'I say, *mpioko!*' called the Terrible One. 'Where did you steal those giant trousers?'

Mwambu was completely taken aback by the unexpected question.

'Did you hear my question?'

'Yes.'

'Not yes, but yes, sir!'

'Yes, sir.'

'Right!' Tortoise butted in. 'And who is your father?'

Mwambu's mind flashed back to his father as he appeared to him on the stone in the middle of the stream…

'They call him papa.'

The entire gang burst out laughing.

'Stupid green leaf!' continued Tortoise. 'I meant, what is his name?'

'His name is Animal,' said Mwambu cheekily. And they knew he was fooling them.

'Do you know who you are playing with?' flared the Terrible One, clenching his fist and bringing it within two inches of Mwambu's nose. 'Hey,' he repeated, 'do you know that you're playing with hot fire?'

'Yes.'

'Yes, sir! I told you to reply, "Yes, sir"!'

'Yes, sir.'

'That's correct.' And then relenting a little, he said, 'And now let me ask you this one. How many eyes do you have?'

Mwambu very well knew the riddle question. It was a challenging invitation to point out some new or strange object, or somebody approaching. So he replied, 'Two eyes.'

'Correct! And what have you seen?' he went on, mischievously fixing his eyes on the marks the evaporated dew had left on Mwambu's shoulders.

'What have I seen? Where?'

Another burst of laughter from the bullying gang. The thing was where he could never see.

'People,' said Tortoise, '*mpioko* has made me laugh till my legbone is bent!'

'Mine, too,' added Double-Eater. 'But I say, maybe he has only *one* eye?'

'Oh no, he has two,' protested the Terrible One with mock conviction. 'You have two eyes, not so? What have you seen with them?'

Mwambu was beginning to lose his temper. This was not a game but harassment for their own fun. He looked away and answered, 'Nothing.'

'Nothing!' threatened Terrible One. 'Nothing! Well, I'm not surprised. But have you ever seen water?'

'Yes,' Mwambu quickly answered, somewhat intrigued by the childishly simple question. And he thought: *Water in the stream. In the fountain. In the sky. In mud puddles in which he and Khalayi loved to play after rain. In...*

'And where have you seen it?'

'In the water-pot,' came the ready answer.

Again the interrogating trio burst into laughter, real enjoyable laughter. He had not seen water in some big river but in a water-pot! And Mwambu was thinking of the many times he had been to the clay water-pot in his house, either to draw water, or to call his mother, when she was away, by speaking into it:

'Please mother come home
I am hungry and lonely.'

And sure as sunrise she would appear within no time, carrying firewood or a bunch of *matooke* or a basket of vegetables or another pot of water.

'And yet,' aimed the Terrible One, after his comrades-in-fun had laughed their fill, 'with so much water in your father's house you have never thought of scrubbing your spotted shoulders!'

At last the truth at his back broke upon him – the point behind the questioning. He felt like madly striking at them or…

But a bell sharply and abruptly ended the break and saved things. A woman in a white dress peeped out of a classroom window and shouted, 'Come on, you boys! Why are you crowding around the new boy? In you go, double quick!'

The following day Mwambu learnt that the lady in white was Mrs Nabwera, the wife of the headmaster. And later in the week she came to his class to teach about the Creator. That was her subject. And Numbers. The Creator and Numbers. And whenever she came to teach his class he paid the utmost attention, out of his secret liking for her. And she taught such wonderful things, told such wonderful stories.

She taught them that the Creator can do things and then rub them out. And that if any of the pupils did bad things and said sorry the Creator would rub those things out. Like she was going to rub out her own writing from the blackboard. She scribbled some nonsensical thing on the board and rubbed it out…

When the Creator does that, she said, we call it forgive-ness. He rubs the thing out so that it is no longer there. He subtracts the bad action from yesterday! So that yesterday or last year is less by that bad action! Like three mangoes, of which one is rotten. If you take away the rotten one and throw it into a fire, you have only two good ones left and you cannot have the bad one back again. The bad mango becomes nothing after burning, like the writing she had rubbed out – or could any of them ever bring it back on to the blackboard?

Mwambu listened with half-open mouth.

And the Creator, she said, can sometimes do certain things himself and then rub them out. He says sorry to himself and subtracts that action from himself!

The rainbow. It had not always been there, she said. Then one day the Creator was angry with all the people because of the very bad things which they had done. So he ordered a torrent of rainwater to cover all the valleys and mountains. And all the people and all the land creatures died. All the men and women and their little ones. All died except one household of good people, whom the Creator had himself warned to build a big, big boat and to hide in it. But after the so many beautiful but bad people had died, the Creator said, I am sorry to myself, because of what I have done. Never again will I kill off my people like this, however bad they become. I swear this day. I swear by myself. And just in case I forget what I have sworn, today I add the rainbow to the sky. Every time I am angry with my people and I see the rainbow, I shall remember my new plan and rub out my anger. And subtract my anger from myself.

'The rainbow,' said Mrs Nabwera, 'is the latest thing that the Creator caused to come into the world.' And she concluded: 'The rainbow is the Creator's reminder.'

The rainbow is the Creator's reminder – Mwambu committed that to memory. It struck him as so beautiful. And the insidemost part of him was aflutter with the novelty of what he had heard. Pulsations of delight in the ancient origin of the many-coloured rainbow.

Ah, yes, it was as his mother had told him. That when the rain was threatening to pour down in a great torrent and a rainbow appears in the sky, that rain does not fall! And time and again, he had seen this truth. Suddenly whenever there appeared two resplendent, never-touching rainbow arcs spanning the mountain face, he knew that the downpour had been cancelled, withdrawn. Most certainly withdrawn for that day. And the clouds lifted and the afternoon sun emerged from the gloom and resumed its radiant mastery of the sky. Ah, the rainbow and the sun! The rainbow and the rain!

But there was a day that he would never forget because of the way his mother had scared him. He and Kangala had gone down to the fountain to draw water by themselves. As they were starting to come back his mother came running down and shouting frantically: 'Away from the water! Quick! Quick! The rainbow has appeared! If you're too near the stream it'll suck you up together with the stream! Come away with me quickly.'

She whisked the water-pot from Mwambu and bid the two boys run ahead of her. After a terrified backward glance at the rainbow, Mwambu ran on without daring to look back again. And for the rest of the day he was deeply troubled by the knowledge that the rainbow can suck up somebody's body.

That very night he had a horrible nightmare in which he encountered a blood-sucking ogre. He had left home at dusk while the rest of the clan was drinking millet brew outside his father's house. Everybody asked him where he was going and he replied that he was just taking a walk. And each of them in turn said he should not take a walk so late, that he might meet horror on the way. But he said he was going and did so. No sooner had he left than he found himself in a trackless jungle, and a spectral monster with countless eyes and the beak of a vulture jumped into his way and started pecking at him and sucking his blood. He tried to run away but for some reason he just kept on running on the same spot. However much he tried to break loose and bolt away he simply felt tied down – transfixed and agonising – far, far away from any human help. He remembered the words of all his clansmen, that he might meet horror on the way, and he cried to himself in words of a song he had learnt from his mother, and which now seemed to spring from an ageless, bottom layer of his young being:

Mother told me Mwambu
> There is horror on the road
Father told me Mwambu
> There is horror on the road...


But I did not listen


Today woe to me Mwambu
Today woe to me


For I did not listen


Though I blow the flute the flute
> There is no rescue
Though I blast the horn the horn
> There is no rescue
Though I strike the gong the gong
> There is no rescue
Though I smite the drum the drum
> There is no rescue


Today woe to me Mwambu
Today woe to me


For I did not listen...


The ogre sucked so much blood from his body that he

started to feel weak all over. He felt himself shrivelling up and beginning to die slowly, slowly...

But mercifully he suddenly woke up from sleep and the horrible nightmare, shaken and angry about his inability to run in the dream. His blanket had been unconsciously thrown off while he slept, his uncovered face turned upwards and his legs doubled up in his bed. Did he have that bad dream because he was naked? he wondered.

In the morning he told his parents his dream. They said it was a very bad dream. And he asked, 'Was I singing or crying in my sleep?' They replied that they had not heard anything.

His mother went to the water-pot and drew water with a calabash. Pouring some into her cupped right hand, she sprinkled the chilling water onto Mwambu without prior warning. He shuddered and looked at her with puzzled eyes.

'Mother, why throw water on me?'

'To drive away the ill luck of your bad dream,' she explained.

And apparently content with the answer, he went on, 'But suppose I had died in my dream, would I have woken up?'

'Yes,' answered his mother. 'To die in a dream is not to die in waking life. It is not to die real death.'

'But,' pursued Mwambu, 'why could I not run in my dream?'

'Because,' replied his father, 'you slept with your legs doubled up. When you sleep like that you cannot run in your dreams. You run on the spot when there is danger. So you must always sleep with your legs stretched out if you do not want bad dreams.'

And now after the rainbow lesson he mixed his present joy with his remembered terror.

*Chapter Four*

At the end of the year many parents came to the school. And his father and mother came. Mrs Nabwera had made him learn certain words by heart and said he would repeat them to the parents. And the words were in the language of his people. She said she had translated them from the red man's *fotifoti* in her simple way, and that if someone translated them back into *fotifoti* they might sound so different.

Mrs Nabwera made him stand in front of the parents, and he was blind with nervousness. Yes, he was blind: he did not look to see where his parents were, nor could he tell afterwards what any of the parents in the front row were wearing. All the eyes of the parents became one giant eye looking down on him from somewhere up there. So he started without breath and recited at a runaway speed:

'Happy is the man among men
         who does not listen to the words of
         the crooked

who does not walk the same path with
lazy-bodies or sit in a circle
with the scornful

For his rejoicing is in what the Creator
approves
and on that does he ponder all day
and night

He is like a fruit-bearing tree
planted by rivers of abundant water
that yields its fruit in the
expected season
and its leaves never dry or fade—
such a man shall always prosper

But not so with those who delight in evil
they are like the millet chaff
that the wind blows with ease

They shall not stand still
when the Creator roars in judgement
nor appear in the assembly of the
blameless

For the Creator is himself in charge
of the path travelled by virtuous
men

but as for the promoters of evil
they are rushing to their doom.'

As soon as he finished, the giant eye of the parents split into many twos of the normal size of human eyes and each two went back to its face. There was a long applause while Mrs Nabwera led him out of the hall. Outside he wedged his way into the crowd of other pupils to hide his face and his excitement.

On first lifting his eyes from the ground, they precisely met with those of Wayero the Terrible One. What bad luck! thought Mwambu. Since that bullying on his first day at the school, Mwambu had never got on well with Wayero, while the other members of the bullying squad had become quite friendly. Pouting his mouth at Mwambu as their eyes met, Wayero said, 'That was not *bad*.'

But Mwambu was still enjoying the after-feeling of his public performance and so he ignored Wayero completely. Wayero was silently placed in the circle of the scornful in the recitation. *But not so with those who delight in evil, they are like millet chaff...*

'I said that was not bad, *mpioko!* All right?'

*But my delight is in what the Creator approves... such a man shall always prosper... but as for the promoters of evil... they are rushing to their doom.... For the Creator is himself in charge of the path...*

Mwambu had wondered about those words when he was first made to repeat them: about the Creator being in charge of a path. And now he wondered about them again. How can he look after a path? Supposing it was very long? Would he be in one place or everywhere on the path? How? Or only at bad points on the path? What if he forgot to guard one of the points…? Oh, then, oh then, maybe the traveller would meet with an ogre! And he would cry for help in vain…

He forced his ears to listen to what was being said in the hall, but there was too much noise outside.

The Headmaster was now delivering his Parents' Day speech. He thanked the parents for their most welcome co-operation in sending their children to the school and for toiling in the fields to raise school fees. But, he said, that was not enough. Not enough children were willing to be released by their parents to go to school.

And the reason for this, he pronounced, was lack of ambition. They were too contented with their mountain spirit. And that spirit, he said, was their excessive pride in their manhood! 'How dare you say that to me, a man?' That was the spirit, and it led nowhere. Not even to a Vernacular Teacher Training College. But the true manhood of the future, he concluded, was the manhood of the brain, of exchanging the spear for the pen. He thanked the parents again and sat down.

While the Headmaster had been speaking, Masaaba was rather wistfully reminded of the trick – of which he was to tell Mwambu years later – that was played by his mother to protect him from joining school in his own day. N.A.C. Namwombe Primary School had just been started. Accompanied by the local chiefs, the two teachers from Buganda went on a countryside campaign to recruit pupils. When they came to the home of Nabutiru, Masaaba's mother, they spied young Masaaba and laid their hands on him, meaning to drag him to school with or without his mother's consent. But Nabutiru pleaded with them to have pity on her old age and spare her last-born child to look after her and her animals. One of the chiefs and the two teachers took her aside. The chief told her that they were willing to listen to her plea but that she must understand that a man does not eat nothing. Then changing the metaphor from food to drink, the chief asked, 'Where is our tea?' After some haggling the bargain was struck. They took two hens and Masaaba was permanently written off. Although he was only ten years old, an entry was made in the Pupils' Recruitment Register to the effect that in the home of Nabutiru, the widow of Watambebumbi son of Wakubona of Musibanga village, there was no child of school-going age. Afterwards Nabutiru repeated the story of her simple negotiation to the village women and they all laughed with warm derision at the greed and pretence of these luggage-carriers of the red man.

Now, walking home with Mwambu and other parents with their children, Masaaba was complimented by fellow-parents on his son's performance as if it was his own. Oh, he had such a good memory. Oh, he would grow up to be a great speaker or a big chief. Oh, he would read all the books and finish them at Makerere. Yes, he would surely read all the books and finish them. And overhearing these wayside remarks, Mwambu was transported into that predicted future of vague, lofty achievements. A future of all books read, and so much else…

The following day was the end of the school year. The pupils hung about in small groups on the grass, anxiously conjecturing whether they had passed or failed their respective examinations. Concealed in the satchels of the toughs were stones and reed-canes for what was known as 'beating you *fainolo.*' On the final day of a term it was a common practice for some pupil to roguishly walk up to another pupil with whom he felt he had a score to settle and to deal him an unsolicited blow in the face or give him a quick lash of the cane, then quickly run home. Some of the pupils were taken unawares while the real toughs never forgot to avail themselves of the pleasure of *fainolo.*

Around midday the bell rang for everybody to report to his class for the examination results and for the dismissal. In Primary One, stream A, there were only two casualties: a boy called Khawanga and, once again, Wayero the Terrible One! Khawanga burst out crying on hearing his name read 'below the red line' but Wayero kept his countenance. Reports were given out and as soon as the class was dismissed Wayero ran out ahead of everybody, firmly holding his satchel under the armpit, and stopped by the corner of the classroom block. Excited pupils were tumbling out of the classrooms and converging and mingling on the grass, congratulating one another upon their passes. Then they started filing away homewards in various directions.

The opportune moment came. Mwambu was just turning the corner in the company of his fellows when Wayero suddenly swished a reed-cane from his side and cracked him across the shoulders. He winced with acute pain. Meanwhile Wayero started running away. Quickly reaching for a large piece of brick from the edge of the flower-garden, Mwambu aimed at his assailant's skull but caught him in the right leg. The leg jacked up and Wayero slumped down, howling like a wounded dog. But in no time he pulled himself up and started limping back towards Mwambu, meaning to finish him off by breaking his neck with his bare hands. But a bigger boy in Primary Four saw that this was threatening to become more than *fainolo* and shouted to Mwambu to run on along with him. And as they increasingly put distance between him and themselves, Wayero shouted obscenities and challenges to a man-on-man combat.

'Don't run away, you coward! I say, you *mpioko*, go and eat shit…! Go and lie on your mother!'

Mwambu stopped. This was too much about his mother. He must go back and fight Wayero, even if he suddenly became ten times bigger. He was going to kill him.

But the wise and friendly bigger boy hauled him along.

And Wayero shouted on: 'Why don't you stop, you coward! Stop if you're a man! I say, you foolish green leaf…

I will get you next year… Just you wait and see. I will show you next year…'

'Yes,' Mwambu too angrily wished, 'let next year come!' He would show Wayero. He would break his skull. He carried that promise inside him. The promise of a war. And in his right hand he carried his report bearing the important words: 'Third Term… Promoted to Primary Two.'

*Chapter Five*

Nerima was a growing village beauty about two years older than Mwambu. She was the daughter of Wopata, Mukimba's brother. Her younger brother Wabwire was of the same age as Mwambu.

Already Nerima was beginning to look more of a woman than a child. Her embryonic breasts had, over the past moons, started swelling into pointed, provocative fruitlets. And the village women had always said that she would be Mwambu's wife. One afternoon during Mwambu's first long vacation, the two met on a hillside path by sheer luck and she could not hide her joy.

After they had greeted each other she said, 'Mwambu, I hear you're very clever at school. Are you going to forget me?'

'I don't think I'm clever,' replied Mwambu. 'But who says that clever people are very forgetful?'

'Oh don't be *clever*!' she snapped sweetly. 'I didn't say that. I mean that you're going to forget me because I'm not in school with you.'

'But I thought that you were at Kangala's school?'

'So you call it Kangala's school? I don't call it a school. It's a tree.'

They laughed pleasantly.

'But it's a school all the same. Anyway, if you don't like it, why don't you come to Namwombe next year?'

'My father says that would cost too much money. He just wants me to get a new name and then stop schooling. So you can forget me as soon as I stop going to that tree you call a school.'

'But why are you saying I'm going to forget you?' asked Mwambu rather impatiently. 'Perhaps you're yourself cunningly thinking of ways to forget me.'

She felt like slapping him. She always felt herself to be in command. When they were much smaller she used to order him to do this and that. 'Jump on my back,' she often said, crouching down, and he would jump on her back. Then she would scurry about with him, calling him her baby, and finally putting him down, she would hug him and abruptly run away.

But what they loved most then was sliding down an anthill upon a banana-stem, and singing '*Nakitumba aloma*,' the song about what Nakitumba, the wise hunchback, warned men concerning other people's property. Mwambu and Nerima might be playing, then he might happen to tickle her or to touch her funny-funny. She would quickly jump aside and encouragingly protest, 'Ee, Nakitumba warned!' And upon that cue they would sing and dance together, keeping more than arm's length to show that they believed what they were reciting:

'Nakitumba warned
Another's property is for the eye
Do not seethe with envy
It has to be given you
Before you can eat it
And eat it with relish

Cut me a propped banana
Let me take it to my mother
Then I will return for *tyekule*

*Tyekule tyekule*
*Tyekule tyekule*
*Tyekule tyekule…*'

And how they enjoyed the sound of *tyekule* upon their tongues. *Khutyekula* was not only to dance with happy youthful steps such as theirs, but it also surely sounded so good!

But with Kangala, Mwambu talked about different things. They talked about different things and planned to do them. Kangala knew Mwambu was fond of pretty little Nerima and often teased him about her.

The day following Mwambu's meeting with Nerima on

the hillside, Mwambu and Kangala went out walking and talking.

'Hey, Mwambu,' Kangala suddenly said, digressing from their present subject of sports. 'Mwambu, yesterday I saw you!'

'You saw me what?' asked Mwambu.

'I saw you with Nerima. At nightfall.'

'Yes, you did,' agreed Mwambu. 'Returning from the hillside where we just met.'

'Where you just met?' queried Kangala, looking sideways at Mwambu. 'I can see you're going to be my brother-in-law very soon.'

Mwambu knew Kangala was only joking.

'But let me tell you, Mwambu,' Kangala carried on in a more serious tone. 'You must be careful about going in for small girls. It is better to test yourself on big, grown-up women.'

After talking around the matter for quite some time, they concluded by agreeing that the easiest women to attempt were the big married ones. Very many of them were report-ed to be fond of young cockerels like themselves. There was that young wife of Mayeku's, for instance. Mayeku was so old and she was so young. She had a standard joke for all the men. Whenever a man greeted her, 'Peace upon you, wife of Mayeku,' she always laughingly replied, 'Who tells you I'm wife of Mayeku? I'm wife of everybody!'

Kangala and Mwambu were walking together a week later when Mayeku's wife met them. She was going to the fountain with her water-pot delicately balanced on her head and was humming a pleasant tune as she came down. The two quickly conferred together in whispers. Then Kangala stepped aside while Mwambu stayed on the path. As she came up to them, they said together – while Mwambu stretched out his hand to her – 'Peace be upon you, wife of everybody.'

'What!' she flared. 'Peace upon *who?* Peace upon wife of *who*, you bedbugs? Away with you! What impudence!'

She put her water-pot down and angrily reached for a nearby dry twig. Seeing, to their utter surprise, that it was turning out to be a murderous response, Kangala and Mwambu hopped off and started running while she shouted furiously after them, 'Never you cross my way with your insolent manners! Do you hear, you young rascals? Never you come near me with the mess under your foreskins!'

They heard the obscenity loud and clear. Later on they agreed that they had miscalculated their first step, and that it was terrible that she considered them to be nobodies. And they concluded that they might always be at a disadvantage as long as they carried upon them that mess that she so abhorred.

## Chapter Six

Although Masaaba was generally known in his own village and nearby villages as a very kind and humorous person, he was also feared for his bad temper. If you aroused that temper of his he did not talk with you twice. He did not even grant you that you were a fellow man, nor would he just use his tongue on you, as verbal quarrels were for women. In the event of being provoked, he preferred to have immediate recourse to his palms and fists and arm muscles, or even leg muscles. Being a powerfully built man, he simply jumped on you, or flung you down upon your back and dealt you several blows before stopping to listen to the pleas of any peacemakers. But occasionally he made the mistake of jumping upon his equal in strength or temper and then there was a fair exchange of fists.

His popular nickname was Kapuru, that is to say, Boer. And he was as much a Kapuru outside his own house as he was inside it. Mwambu and Khalayi lived in readiness for a smacking or caning anytime. And as for Nabusulwa, their mother, although he was very tender to her most of the time, hardly two moons passed before the neighbours heard her crying and shouting, 'This one is killing me for nothing!' Very often it was over some trifle like her giving him hot water to wash himself when he thought it should just be lukewarm. Was he to wait indefinitely outside in the dark, naked as when his mother gave him birth, while the water took its time to cool? And the neighbours said that Nabusulwa might have left him long ago but that she was a good woman. She held firmly to the central pillar of the house against all buffetings, as strongly enjoined to do by her womenfolk before her marriage night.

Some time back Wabwire, Kangala's cousin, had carelessly let cattle wander ahead of him into Masaaba's *matooke* field. A boy Wabwire was playing with saw Masaaba furiously driving the animals back and warned Wabwire. He tried to run away but Masaaba caught up with him after a short distance. He flung him down and thrashed him with a crude stick indiscriminately all over. Though a big boy, and even taller than Mwambu, Wabwire screamed like a girl, and eventually fled home with a sprained wrist and a bleeding nose.

Shortly afterwards there was a small procession to Masaaba's house. It was headed by Wopata, wearing a resolute face and carrying a big club in his right hand. The bulk of the procession comprised excited small children who expected some unusual entertainment. Mukimba and Kuloba made up the rear, and some distance behind them two other adults were casually heading in the same direction on their own pursuits.

Wopata angrily burst into Masaaba's courtyard.

'Come out of the house if you're a man!' he bellowed. Wopata was a muscular and thick-set short man, and Masaaba's own *makooki*, circumcised in the same year.

Masaaba came out fearless and unarmed. He saw the chastised Wabwire cowering behind his father, still sulking.

'Tell me, you brave man,' demanded Wopata, indicating Wabwire with his club, 'is this boy your wife or my son?'

'That's not a fair question,' replied Masaaba sardonically, trying to hold his own temper in check.

'I say, did you mistake my son for your wife there when you were beating him?' Wopata was seething with rage and waving his club about. The other two adults had by now arrived at Masaaba's house. They were men of a neighbouring village and looked on with grave faces.

'*Makooki*,' said Masaaba in a persuasive and conciliatory tone, 'do not speak abominations! I know who my wife is. This boy is our son who…'

'*Our* son indeed! Do you beat up your own son there like that? Do you beat him with the intention of killing him? That's your son there, and this is my son. We have no common son, no common wife. That there is your wife. Beat her up. Beat her more often than you have done in the past whenever you feel mad, not other men's children! If you're a manly man you should wrestle with another man, not break the bones of a mere boy. That's not bravery but cowardice. It's worse than beating a woman, which is your major work. And don't fool me, don't fool yourself by calling me *makooki!* It's an insult to me, after beating up my child like that.'

'Well,' interposed Mukimba, 'you are *bamakooki* all the same. You can't remove that and that's not what you're quarrelling about.'

'Is it not what we are quarrelling about?' returned Wopata, unabated. 'He talks of speaking abominations. If he was my *makooki* would he not know that it's an abomination for him to beat my son or to touch my daughter? Does he also want me to go and bring him my daughter Nerima to lie with him?'

'*Puch!*' shouted all the grown-ups. '*Puch!* Wopata, how are you speaking? *Puch!* Do you want to destroy Nerima?'

Mwambu was so amazed at the sudden spoken idea of Nerima lying with his father!

'Wopata,' rallied Masaaba, now letting his temper go, 'you've called me mad already. But if it's madness to cane an insolent boy who so often lets your cattle loose upon my crops, what is it to be the father of such a boy? It's foolishness. Do you hear that? It's foolishness like that of a woman!'

Wopata came at Masaaba with his club raised high while Masaaba got ready to stave off or grab the club. But very quickly Mukimba and Kuloba jumped into Wopata's way. After some struggle the two fuming *bamakooki* were persuaded to restrain themselves and behave like grown-up, circumcised men.

'Then, Mukimba,' said Masaaba, 'tell your brother that

he's a circumcised man and I'm a circumcised man. Let him keep out of my courtyard. If he has a serious matter to settle with me, he must trot all the way to the sub-county headquarters at Namwombe and beat his tail down like a dog before the chief. After all, the red man's rule came to protect such cowards. Mukimba, tell him that. That he must never come into my courtyard again brandishing that club of his. Is it this porridge of a son that he comes to brag to me about in my own courtyard?'

'Old one,' said Kuloba to Masaaba, 'please don't start the quarrel all over again.'

'No, Kuloba. But you can also look and wonder. He tells the boy to graze his beasts upon my crops and then brings him here to show him off! And he says that I must not call him *makooki*. Now by the knife that ate me, I swear that on the day this boy stands upon Wopata's courtyard they will send to inquire from me whether his father and I are *bamakooki* or I just claim it. If I am joking then I did not stand the pain in the year of locusts.'

'Masaaba,' counselled Mukimba, 'that's not a kind threat. You're speaking dangerous words out of anger. Supposing your words fall onto the ground and germinate? What you're saying is not good.'

'Let him say what he likes,' said Wopata. 'I only came to show him that the only people his itching hand has a right to beat are his wife and children.'

'We've heard that already,' replied Mukimba. 'Can't you stop there?'

'No. He's threatening curses. But he that kills an *Etesot* must replace him with his own kinsman. I have a son, and he has a son...'

Mwambu and Wabwire instinctively looked up and then looked away in mutual embarrassment.

'... there! His is the child of the red ones; mine stays here with me in darkness. But it was the knife of Kisyang'ani that cut me into a man, and by the pain of that knife, I swear that before his son is clothed with the robe of a man I will have to know of it. If I'm telling you mere nonsense, then Masaaba is the only man who stood the pain in the year of locusts!'

Upon that note the quarrelsome meeting ended. Wopata placed his club upon his shoulder and walked away, followed by Wabwire and the village children, who had greatly enjoyed the spectacle of two grown-ups exchanging such hot words. Mukimba and Kuloba stayed on a while after Masaaba had disappeared into the house. They tried to talk to Nabusulwa about some irrelevant commonplace matters, to take her mind away from the day's incident. They knew how careful she had to be for the rest of the day, for upon the smallest provocation, or even none, Masaaba would be on her neck to rid himself of the rest of his anger.

Mwambu aimlessly walked about the courtyard, feeling personally beaten down because of that quarrel. He had not understood all that had been said but he felt some kind of premonition. Why did his father have to quarrel with Nerima's father? Would Kangala and Wabwire stop speaking to him because of what had happened?

While Mwambu was lost in these dark thoughts Masaaba re-emerged from the house and said to him, 'Mwambu, come with me for a walk. You must see the damage that led to this foolish talk of Wopata's. That plot of young *matooke* suckers is hardly there. Come with me.'

*Chapter Seven*

The following year the declared war between Wayero and Mwambu did not take place. Their sharply defined intention had been dulled by their long absence from each other. And then for a long time thereafter there occurred no strong pretext to provoke an armed struggle. So for the time being they contented themselves with looking at each other like dog and sheep whenever their paths crossed.

Then one day, in the course of the year, the Headmaster caused the school drum to be frantically beaten to summon everyone together instantly. All the pupils instinctively knew that particular, urgent rhythm. It said:

'Singana umurakaraki
Singana umurakaraki
Singana umurakaraki...'

[I don't like the indolent
I don't like the indolent
I don't like the indolent...]

They came running out of the classrooms, and when they had assembled on the grass the Headmaster made his announcement: 'I have a letter here from the District Commissioner in Elgonton to tell you all at once that the war of the whole world has broken out!'

Some of the younger children burst into loud laughter, while the older pupils and the teachers tried to look grave and worried to show that they knew perfectly well what it all meant.

The Headmaster went on to explain that the whole world was divided into two warring armies: British and German. The British, he said, were fighting for right, and the Germans were fighting for wrong. The Protectorate of Uganda was going to fight on the side of right and the British against the Germans, who were very bad, cruel and greedy people, and were intending to force their way into the Protectorate and kill everybody. So they had to be cut off and destroyed in a certain far away desert country.

Ah, regretted Mwambu, the war of the whole world had broken out and he could not see it! He could not hear the ecstatic war cry and see the glinting spear blades as stalwart warriors dashed across the battlefield in complex ever-changing formation of men and their shields. There were desert and forest countries, they said, beyond the mountain and that plain, beyond the reach of the eye. Very, very far away. When the sun rose in the morning, it was setting in Buyindi, the land of the yellow men.

When it set in the evening, it was rising in Bulaya, the land of red men. And numberless yellow men and red men all lived on this same earth, which was so big and round and always spinning and speeding away in endless sky, faster than a catapulted stone, with the sun and the moon and the stars. All this, the teacher said, was true but you could not see it because a man standing upon the earth was like the tiniest insect on a football. The insect could never tell that the football was round or when it was rolling!

War had broken out in the land of red men and it was spreading across to the land of yellow men, the teacher said. Across deserts and forests and seas.

Then surely, thought Mwambu, that must be the land of long, long ago to which monsters used to whisk men to eat them.

Only the week before he had told his class a story with such a monster in it. It was a story retold by his mother many times:

'... Then one day while Monster was out in the field, Sera slipped out of her prison-house and fled upon wings of the wind towards home. When Monster returned from work he discovered that she had escaped and gave chase. Meanwhile Sera came across Frog and begged her to hide her in her belly so that Monster may not see her. Failing to descry Sera his side of the horizon, Monster decided to make use of his elastic magic belt to catch her. He flung it ahead of him with a mighty thrust:

"Tchuku-tchuku-tchuku-tchuku…

Tsyomulye tsyomulye tsyomulye…"

[Go eat 't 't 't her…]

'The belt leapt forward in gigantic snake-like folds across the rivers of the plain. It got hold of Frog and retracted to Monster with Frog in one of its folds.

"You sly Frog!" shouted Monster. "You have hidden Sera!"

"Not I!" Frog protested.

"Yes, you have, you liar! Open your mouth."

'But Frog had cleverly hidden Sera in a dark corner of her belly, so when Monster looked into her mouth, Frog just brought up white slime. The sight was so sickening that Monster instantly closed his eyes and shouted, "*Poh poh poh!* Shut your foul mouth quickly!"

'Frog shut her mouth and was returned upon the magic belt to the spot from which she had been picked. Three times Monster flung his magic belt forward. And every time it was Frog it caught, and each time Frog performed her trick of bringing up the sickening slime.

'In the end Monster gave up the chase.

'At sunset Frog hopped into Sera's father's courtyard. All the relatives were gathered there to perform the last death rites of Sera, who, they had concluded, must have been devoured by Monster. Frog made as if to enter the house together with the homecoming chicken but one kinsman shouted her aside. But calling her by her pet-name, Sera's mother said that Namakanda, or the Lady of Beans, must not be thrown out as she was always mankind's friend. So Frog hopped into the house and stopped behind the water-pot and was given some food by Sera's mother. After she had eaten her fill, she drew everybody's attention by suddenly claiming that she was going to make the clan a very beautiful gift. Then opening her mouth, as if to ungratefully throw up what she had just eaten, she vomited out a smiling and healthy-looking Sera…!'

After Mwambu had retold the story, the teacher remarked: 'Nowadays Frog is the red man's automobile. You can be so cleverly tucked away in its boot that no friend or enemy searching the front will see you!'

The war years were marked by the marching band at Namwombe. Every Friday morning school started with assembly. Each class lined up behind the class-leader in three rows in ascending order of height.

The girls were extracted from their respective classes and organised into two groups, senior and junior. The band then struck up and you marched to its martial music of drums and flutes intermingled with bugles and rattles. Every last Friday in the month you marched the entire one mile to Namwombe sub-county headquarters, bringing the salutations of the centre of learning to the seat of government. And the village children came out and lined the road, admiring and envying you in your smart khaki uniforms so specially ironed for the impressive day that your sharp trouser creases could 'cut a fly'.

And on the return journey, as you neared the school, marching up the gentle, green slope, oh you liked yourselves and liked life and liked your being young and liked N.A.C. Namwombe Primary School! The band always played a favourite closing tune, and you whistled or hummed with all the instruments as they combined to say:

'This is Namwombe

Our good clean school

This is Namwombe

Our good clean school.'

And the rhythm said: 'Left, right, left, right... Enjoy it all! Enjoy it now!'

Then, as your class arrived opposite members of staff standing with the Headmaster outside the classrooms, your leader shouted in a strong military voice:

'Eye------s right!'

And you all simultaneously did four co-ordinated things: clamped hands to your sides with a noisy *'pah!'*; brought feet together in a temporary halt; turned head sharply right to fix eyes on the Headmaster; then you resumed the march forward in unbroken formation. Eyes not looking where you were going and hands pointing stiffly downwards like penguin wings! After some dozen paces the leader shouted your release:

'Eye-----s front!'

You now looked ahead and swung your arms freely and marched the last bit of the road before turning at right angles into your assembly lot.

When all the classes were back, the master-on-duty announced the best and most militant marchers of the day to the applause of all. You then stood at attention as the band played 'God Save Our Gracious King' before dismissal. The gracious king, the Headmaster had explained when the anthem was first played, was King George VI, to be saved from a certain terrible madman called Hitler and his murderous tribesmen.

Before the war ended, that National Anthem prayer was practically and locally answered: a number of old boys of Namwombe were recruited into the King's African Rifles, known as KEYA, to defend King George VI and the British flag on four continents and various islands. Two years before the war was over even Kunikina the Tortoise was called up. He had left school after reaching Primary Six and was now in his late teens and living in the village.

The same year, returning from school one day through an afternoon drizzle, Mwambu was hit by news of conscription in his own village. Khalayi, who was now a fast-growing girl of seven attending the village school, skipped to meet him.

'Mwambu,' she said excitedly, 'they've taken away Kuloba.'

'Taken him where?'

'To Elgonton to fight the Germans.'

'Germans are not in Elgonton. That's only twenty miles away. But why are you lying to me?'

'I'm not lying.'

'You swear that Kuloba is not at home.'

'*Matsima ni kwoku!*' she said, spitting into her right palm and raising the hand to the sky.

In the house his mother confirmed Khalayi's news. And Mwambu was both happy and sad that his cousin had gone to join the war. Happy and envious in imagining Kuloba wielding the fabulous gun in some desert country and slaughtering a hundred German monsters. And sad because Patrick Kuloba was his favourite cousin and he was now away. And because Mwambu had asked him to be present at his forthcoming christening ceremony.

*Chapter Eight*

Clad in immaculately white dresses or white shirts and trousers with white canvas shoes, their heads shaven to egg-smoothness, the candidates knelt in penitent pews. They had visibly taken heed of the advice of some of their predecessors who suggested they cut off their hair otherwise the holy water would not filter through to the spirit beneath but just trickle down the temples.

The baptiser had been a long time preparing them for the great once-and-for-all admission. During this time he made them memorise 'the moral code of the people of God', as he loved to call the Ten Commandments. He also made them weed his *shambas* of *matooke*, coffee and maize. For their own good, he said, for the toughening of body and spirit, in imitation of Christ's deliberate affliction of himself through fasting before starting on his immense work.

The Reverend Matamali, the baptiser, was the parish priest of N.A.C. Namwombe church. Slightly bow-legged, short and stout, he was an ageing man with half-open tortoise eyes and a receding hairline. He was one of the very first batch of indigenous men to become ordained priests at Elgonton Theological College. He particularly enjoyed teaching the catechism to the baptismal candidates, and especially to Mwambu's lot of youngsters whom he sensed to be profitably thirsty for heaven. He loved the conversational style, which gave him a lot of room for padding and adding his personality to the catechism.

'And so who is it that moulded you?'

'It is the moulder that moulded me.'

'Who is it that will pull you to pieces?'

'It is the moulder that will pull me to pieces.'

'Right. Why is it that it is not death that will pull you to pieces?'

'Because death is only a messenger-slave of the moulder.'

'Correct. And where is the moulder to be found?'

'The moulder is to be found in every place.'

'Correct. In every place and in every no-place. Everywhere and everynowhere. Because you can get to the moulder by going nowhere... Heaven itself is not a place but a state of happiness. Where is heaven then?'

'Heaven is wherever the moulder is.'

'Yes. So every time he is in your heart, heaven is right inside you! And where is hell?'

'Hell is in Gehenna.'

'No! Hell is wherever the moulder is not, wherever he is absent. Every time he is not in you, you become a container of hell! And lastly, how many persons are there inside the moulder?'

'Three persons.'

'How many moulders are there inside each person?'

'One moulder.'

'Can any of the three persons go on a journey without the other two?'

'No! Never! The three are always together inside the one moulder.'

The Reverend Matamali was indeed a success with the schoolchildren because of his comic wit and his habit of emphasising the sunny rather than the gloomy side of faith. Christians should sing and shout for joy, he taught, more than they beat their breasts. And the Ten Commandments, he explained, were not ten fetters but ten wide-open exits to freedom from the prison of nature. The thing to aim for, he often advised, was just to love the moulder completely and then to do anything you pleased in heaven and hell and – especially – on earth!

As for a good sermon – he once revealed in words that made Mwambu recall his first Parents' Day recitation – it is that which threshes and sifts the listeners into grain and chaff. Following such a sermon, when all communicants are invited to go up to the Holy Table, some of them sift themselves out as chaff through the back door, and are quickly blown down the road in the direction generally taken by all the husks of this world. He was accordingly nicknamed '*Kusengejja*', that is to say, Mr Sifting. But above all, the schoolchildren thought of him in connection with his amusing mapping of the drunkard's onomatopoeic progress towards his fate – first tiptoeing in for a soda, and then on to beer, to *waragi*, and finally to crude, unpurified *nguuli*:

> Sota akhusotesa
> Pya wakhupyakula
> Waraki wakhwarakaka
> Inguuli yakhukuulisa

> [Soda tip-toes you
> Beer splinters you
> Waragi crashes you
> Nguuli explodes you]

And now the Reverend Matamali Kusengejja was beaming with joy as new infant citizens were ushered into the kingdom of heaven by his right hand. They filed up the aisle, and meekly stepped to the font one by one.

'Zephaniah Wabisiima Masette, I baptise you in the name of the Father and of the Son and of the Holy Spirit. Amen...

'Peter Twaaya Wayero, I baptise you in the name of the Father and of the Son and of the Holy Spirit. Amen...

'Jane Matiinyi Nafula, I baptise you in the name of the Father and of the Son and of the Holy Spirit. Amen...'

Mwambu walked forward with a loudly pumping heart. He was both apprehensive and full of yearning as his wondering thoughts about what it must feel like to be baptised became a thing of the past and the real thing now happened to him…

'Abraham Kiboole Mwambu I baptise you…

*(Sudden trembling vacancy in head and breast)*

'… in the name of the Father…

*(First chilling shiver)*

'… and of the Son…

*(Second shiver)*

'… and of the Holy Spirit…

*(Third shiver)*

'… Amen.

*(Ecstasy and flapping of inner wings!)*

'And I mark you with the sign of the cross…

*(Indelible brand burnt into the forehead, down and across, by the chilling water)*

'… in token that henceforth you shall not be ashamed to confess the faith of Christ and him crucified…

*("Nokusoka abewaffe – Beginning in my home")*

'… and that you will *manfully* fight under his banner…

*(Brandishing flaming spear in the wilderness)*

'… against sin, the world and the devil…

*(Sinking spear into Monster)*

'… and continue Christ's faithful soldier and servant to your life's end. Amen.'

Drums of joy. Sunshine and rainbow. Applause over mountain in highest heaven. Butterfly from chrysalis.

After the service the Reverend Matamali stood at the

door and shook hands in turn with all the new inmates of his sheepfold as they passed out into the world:

'Well done and welcome to the flock, Jane. You're now a child of God.'

'Thank you, Reverend.'

'Well done and welcome to the flock, Peter. The kingdom of heaven is now yours.'

'Thank you, Reverend.'

'Well done and welcome to the flock, Zephaniah. The old things have passed away.'

'Thank you, Reverend.'

'Well done and welcome to the flock Abraham. In Christ you're now a man.'

'Thank you, Reverend.'

'Well done and welcome…'

And outside god-parents and earthly parents and relatives and teachers and well-wishers chorused their felicitations to the various brides of Christ the Lord.

'Congratulations, Abraham.'

'Thank you for your prayers, teacher.' *In Christ I'm now a man.*

'Well escaped the paganism of some of us.'

'It's as you say, mother.' *In Christ I'm now a man.*

'You've done well to buy a new name, Mwambu.'

'Thank you for the two shillings, father,' joked Mwambu. 'But I did not buy Christ with it.' *In Christ I'm now a man.* 'It's to help run the work of the parish.'

'Well, I must not argue with you on your happy day,'

replied Masaaba also in a joking mood and then lowering his voice: 'I must not say that swelling the pocket of a certain somebody in this world is the best way of making the work of the Church run very fast.'

And then a man Mwambu only vaguely recognised as having seen before, half-seriously said, partly to amuse himself, 'Congratulations, Mwambu, on rejecting Satan and all his works!'

And Mwambu politely replied, by way of beginning to witness for Christ with immediate effect, 'And you too for having done the same, or for intending to do so.'

*Chapter Nine*

A nd then the famine came. The harvest was very poor that year because of the worst and longest drought that had ever afflicted the land. For so said old men.

And the sad thing about this famine was that the previous year had been such a rich harvest. Mwambu remembered with delight what an abundant harvest that had been. On the first day of the Second Term holidays he had joined the reapers in Kuloba's millet field. And the whole village came to help: men and women and boys and girls. The men proudly, merrily walked into the field as soon as the dew had evaporated from the laden millet-heads.

And the men told such hearty jokes while you cut the grain, rhythmically bending forward to take in several stalks in one swoop and straightening up as you transferred the stalks to your left hand. When you had cut enough to fill the hand, you pressed the millet-heads compactly together upon the palm of your right hand and cut off the excessive lengths of stalk in one swift stroke of the knife. From time to time Mwambu played the well-known game of propelling the stalks upon the knife-blade towards some unprepared nearby fellow-reaper, just as a bit of show-off.

Then as basket after basket was filled, the women carried the grain homewards, delicately balancing the baskets upon their heads, and talking happily and noisily as they came and went, or singing songs of thankfulness for nature's bounty.

But that was the year before, and now it was a raging famine. People said that it was the red man's war that had brought about this evil luck. For had the war not taken away the young men, they argued, who should be clearing virgin jungle for their wives to cultivate?

From that war occasional news did return of a son or husband who had died on the battlefield, whose bones would never see the ancestral burial ground. Mwambu would shudder at the thought that Kuloba, his dear cousin, might never return. So out of the famine and the war women composed songs of sorrow. They sang them at the grinding stones as they ground their meagre stock of millet. And Mwambu's tears almost rose to the surface whenever his mother and some neighbour woman sang the sad song of Makumbamomu:

'Hold for me this Oh Dry-bones
I go see that crying woman

Is she tear-crying or singing?

She was a wife and a mother
That forlorn crying woman

Is she tear-crying or singing?

She was the mother of a girl so fair
She was the mother of a boy so tall

Is she tear-crying or singing?

She lost her girl to Mutanganyi Famine
She lost her boy to the red man's war

Oh she is tear-crying not singing!'

'But even if this famine continues forever,' announced Kangala to Mwambu, 'next year I must fall. I must be eaten by the knife.'

They were out in the fields just before sunset one evening during Mwambu's Christmas holidays. The two had remained very close friends over the passing years. Kangala had not continued with reading books after completing the village school. He was now in his early youth and a faint moustache was just beginning to germinate upon him.

'I must be eaten by the knife,' Kangala repeated.

'Oh, you sure must!' replied Mwambu. He had never forgotten the cutting marks of Mayeku's wife. The knife would raise them above such taunts of women.

'Wabwire has also resolved to fall. How about you? Or will you fall the following one?'

'Most likely the following one, yes. You are older. And even Wabwire must have eaten one more granary than me.'

'But perhaps you will go to hospital,' teased Kangala. 'You *bazungu* can't bear the courtyard.'

'Of course I can!' Mwambu was slightly vexed by the insult. 'Of course I can, and I will. And please don't call me a *Muzungu*. I'm even blacker than you! I shall fall, or I should say "stand". I shall stand upon the courtyard.'

'Well, if you don't stand,' pursued Kangala sarcastically, enjoying the wordplay, 'you can lie on your back.'

'Kangala, why do you speak bad luck on me? Do you mean I shall fear *imbalu*? I won't.'

'I'm only joking, Mwambu,' returned Kangala, smiling. 'But in hospital they say you lie on your back. First they kill you. Then when you're coming back to life they stretch you out on a wooden board. And then while you're counting the beams in the roof, an *Etesot* doctor circumcises you. You're circumcised by an uncircumcised circumciser! Or even a woman.'

'A woman!' exclaimed Mwambu.

'Yes, Mwambu,' Kangala affirmed coolly. 'A woman. A woman circumciser of womanly men.'

After they had parted, Mwambu continued to feel disturbed for quite a while because of the nasty things Kangala was hinting at. But *imbalu* was not uppermost in his mind that holiday. It was the examinations that he had just sat that were uppermost. 'Please, please, God,' he prayed, 'let me pass my Primary Leaving Examinations. So that I don't return to Namwombe next year. Because I don't want to go back and repeat. I don't want to repeat like Wayero used to repeat every class, before finally dropping out in Primary Three. Please, God…'

*Chapter Ten*

Elgon Secondary School. In short, Elgosec – and its products – Elgonians. First term, and Mwambu coming up from Namwombe. White Sunday best with elastic blue belts and black leather shoes. Brick classroom blocks with red tile roofs. An imposing centrally situated four-wing chapel. Avenues of whispering coniferous trees. A ring of dormitories outskirting the school compound, all named after the major rivers of the mountain: Manafwa, Solokho, Simu, Khamitsaru, and for the girls' hostel, Lwakhakha – meaning 'However-Beautiful-She-Is'. Laboratories with countless bottles of all sizes and shapes. A treasure house of colourful shelves of books, each beckoning to be opened first. A swimming pool of sky-blue water. Games uniforms according to the colours of the various houses: blue, green, yellow, red and violet. Debating Society, Dramatic Society, Christian Union, Science Club, Mountaineering Club… Students from mountain and plains and beyond the horizon. Languages of near and far in glorious mix-up:

'*Aterere, mukhwasi!*'

'*Mwatu ejakait, empaako yaawo?*'

'*Tafadhali unisaidie* by shutting your mandibles!'

'History is the study of by-gone men and their petty or heroic deeds...

'Geography is the study of the earth's face...

'Domestic Science is the art of managing household scarcities...

'Language is vocal articulation of...? Man is an animal which...? God is he that...?'

The Chemistry teacher said, 'Touch it, smell it, taste it (if you're brave), measure it, weigh it, dissolve it in water, heat the outcome, weigh the residue, dissolve it in any acid, observe it...'

'And what do you think,' asked the Language teacher, 'that the author meant by not saying it...?'

Some one hundred feet away from the chapel stood the Tree of God. It was a massive, tall *kumutoto* tree with a broad evergreen canopy, standing on the same level and within the same holy precincts as the chapel, both being fenced in by three rounds of barbed wire. The top wire, said the incorrigibles, was for the Father; the middle one for the Son; and the bottom one for the Holy Spirit. It was called the Tree of God because it was the meeting place of the Christian Union, which congregated under its wings at least twice a week. But it was more emphatically called the Tree of God because it was also the tree of lovers. The Christian Union would meet under it in the hot afternoon; and in the cool of the evening, between supper and prep, pairs of linked shadows could be spied lurking and sneaking under its protective darkness. At the approach of the master-on-duty with torch light the shadows would suddenly disengage and scurry off in the direction of the brightly lit classrooms.

Between them, the two neighbouring houses of God – the concrete and the vegetable – were responsible for the moulding of the students' spiritual vision of themselves. To the concrete shrine every student came by the law of the school; to the vegetable shrine voluntarily came the zealous only. The Deputy Headmaster, the Reverend James Graves, was at once both the chaplain of the man-made house of God and the patron of the natural house of God. And from the very beginning Mwambu went to both sanctuaries.

As the presiding spirit of the Christian Union, the Reverend Graves encouraged the zealous few to always 'walk in the light' and to avoid the trinity of hell: which comprised the three untouchables of smoking, drinking and sexing. The zealous called him Brother James and did not listen to the stories of the unredeemed students to the effect that when the Reverend had guests at his house from his own country he freely partook of the first two untouchables.

Mathematician, theologian and former sportsman, the Reverend Graves was a bespectacled gentleman of medium height in his early fifties at the time Mwambu came up to Elgosec. He was a strong personality, who tended to overshadow the Headmaster, Mr Arthur Bentley. But whereas time was beginning to honour the Reverend Graves with a sprinkling of grey hair upon his balding head – as a token of accumulated wisdom – he did not wish to be thought of as beginning to grow old. He severely reprimanded any student who reverently addressed him as 'Old One' in greeting him. 'I'm not old,' he would fume. 'You must address me as Reverend Graves. Full stop.'

One thing about the Reverend Graves was common knowledge to the students: that his homestead was a graveyard, on account of his wife 'Twiga'. Of tall masculine build, Twiga had a long giraffe neck and long cylindrical legs that thumped the ground like two noisy locomotive pistons. You would know she was heading your way long before she turned the corner of some building and came within your line of vision. She was exactly the kind of wife, the boys joked, who would never find you out when you went stealing, as she could never come upon you unawares. As loud a talker as she was noisy a walker, she was an ultra-critical affliction to the Reverend Graves, who, in loving response, kept away from the house for as long as he could, to minimise friction hours, dividing his prolonged evening leisure between lawn tennis and country dance with the students.

As manageress of the school canteen, Twiga gave Mwambu a very early feel of the rough end of her tongue. Mwambu had started pairing off with lovely Jane Nambozo, a classmate of his, and the two were to be seen often together at both houses of God, in the dining hall and in the library. They went down together to the canteen to buy something to eat on the afternoon of Mwambu's first face-to-face encounter with Twiga.

'Good afternoon, madam,' greeted Mwambu.

She looked him critically up and down through her gold-rimmed spectacles.

'Good afternoon, young man.' Then she continued sternly, 'Must you be the next one to be informed that my name is not Madam? My proper and correct name is Mrs Graves.'

Mwambu was at a complete loss.

'Yes, madam,' he involuntarily agreed.

'Yes, *what?*'

'Yes, madam, I mean, sorry, yes, Mrs Graves.'

He felt very uncomfortable in front of Nambozo.

'"Madam" is a word that in Great Britain is used by shop assistants in addressing their customers. But here in Africa you all think that every woman and every lady is "Madam".'

Mwambu responded with embarrassed silence.

'And what do you want to buy?' she asked, changing the subject.

Mwambu was very sure he said he wanted a cake, there being a whole basket of cakes on the counter.

'Sorry, I don't have any!' she announced very firmly.

Mwambu opened his eyes a little wider and looked at the so many cakes under her very sharp nose.

'And what are these?' he asked, pointing at the cakes.

'Oh, these?' she said, superiorly craning her long neck. 'But you said you wanted a *kek*. These are *keiks*. One of them is a *keik* not a *kek*.'

Mwambu did not have the slightest idea what the august lady was going on about.

'So you do want a *keik?*' she pursued mercilessly.

'Yes, mad—, I mean, Mrs Graves. That's what I still want.'

'What you *still* want!' she fumed. 'No, that's what you *now* want.' Then changing to a milder tone, she declared, 'Well, twenty cents!' And so declaring, she held out her open left hand while her right one descended, rested and waited upon one of the cakes for the duration of Mwambu's extraction of the money from his rather narrow hind pocket. Upon the arrival of the two clinking copper coins into Mrs Graves's left palm, her naked thumb and second finger of her right hand ritually lifted the said cake and transferred it to Mwambu's vexed ownership.

*Chapter Eleven*

But two years later, Kangala and Wabwire were not eaten by the knife as Kangala had previously assured Mwambu. When the time came for the two cousins to commence the season's manhood dance, their parents decided that the young people were still too weak around the elbows and knees and must therefore await the next falling. Kangala and Wabwire had already indeed started on collecting the dance items, beginning with the hand-bells. But they obeyed their parents and let the knife pass by that year. It was then agreed by both the parents and the intending candidates that since in two years' time the two youngsters would have grown into tougher bullocks, they would have to dance the thigh-bells and not hand-bells.

Deprived of the season's festivity at first hand, since his two friends were not going to fall, Mwambu spent most of the August holiday rather indolently. There was not much fun around. Nerima, his childhood wife, had matured ahead of him into a woman and eloped with a maker of musical instruments in Bumbo, where Namisindwa ridge tails off into Kenya. He had recently learnt that she had even given birth to a baby girl already. And he had wistfully thought how she had now become another's property, as they used to sing in Nakitumba song, upon whom only the eye may feed without blame. Oh, but perhaps if they met one day, he thought, he would do as the ancients sing!

*Mambire umwana*
*Inome ni mawe*

[Hold for me the child
And let me talk with its mother]

But he had quickly corrected himself, for would not that be adultery? For he was now a Christian and a child of God. He read his Bible every day and prayed sincerely from deep down for purity of body and spirit. 'Do you not know that your body is a temple of the Holy Ghost?' Mwambu loved those words; that He who was too big and too high for Solomon's Temple now actually lived inside himself! 'For you shall be perfect just as your heavenly Father is perfect… Therefore flee all inordinate and youthful pleasures… Adultery… concupiscence… fornication… let them not be named among you… For if anyone is in Christ he is a new creation!' He had committed those lovely admonitions to memory.

By way of occupying his leisure time Mwambu was developing into a bookworm. Even when he went grazing his father's cattle, instead of carrying a knife or a spear against a possible wild aggressor, he took a book with him. After making sure that the animals were facing in a safe direction, not towards a neighbour's crops, he would settle down under a tree on the grass or on some stone and read a few pages of the book. The villagers got to learn of his habit and said that he was a strange one.

On the second day of the third term holiday that year, a thought came to him that he might go and see that funny Mayuba to while away some of the time talking to her. Kuloba had now been away in the war for three years. The two children had, that morning, gone to visit their grand-mother for some days, and so Mayuba was alone when he arrived. She was peeling a miserable-looking bunch of *matooke*, for famine was still eating people. She was sitting by the doorway, with her legs to one side, and as she peeled the miserable-looking *matooke* she was singing a miserable song and was herself wearing a miserable long-suffering face:

'*Nalinda uwaramayo*
*Wo yaya!*
*Nalinda uwa Keya*
*Wo yaya!*'

[Waiting for the last one to come
O dear me!
Waiting for one who went to war
O dear me!]

On setting her eyes on Mwambu she exclaimed, 'God is there! I was crying for you in song, and just look who walks into my lonely compound!'

Mwambu was very pleased by her enthusiastic lie.

'Am I the awaited one of Keya then?' he asked light-heartedly.

'Come near!' said Mayuba, throwing her peeling knife aside and getting up. 'Come near and let me embrace you and hold you with my dirty hands. Oh, I am so lucky today. You see, I didn't even know that you were back from school.'

After they had embraced she still held him around the waist.

'Oh, lucky me!' she repeated. 'You're now such a tall husband! Taller than me, which is very good. I don't want a husband to be shorter than me.'

'Why not?' asked Mwambu, enjoying it.

'Because when we're quarrelling I can bite him on the head.'

'So you would rather it's your husband who bites you on the head?'

'Oh no,' she said, releasing him and beckoning him to a chair. 'However tall he is he should not bite me on the head. That would be very unmanly of him.'

'Well,' returned Mwambu, 'however tall a woman is she should never bite her husband on the head. That would be very unwomanly of her.'

'Not at all! It's not unwomanly. If a man is too short he

deserves it. Because he should not quarrel with his wife. And he should not marry her if she is too tall.'

They laughed merrily together.

Mayuba was by nature a jovial woman. She had a pleasantly insolent and disarming manner. Mwambu was often embarrassed by her because of her jokes that sounded too much like the truth. If she disliked you or thought you were a fool she might tell you, 'As I am Mayuba, you are really a handsome fool!'

They talked about many commonplace things while she finished peeling, washed the *matooke* and took them into the kitchen.

It was beginning to grow dark, so Mwambu stood up to indicate that he must be leaving. She came up to him as if she wanted to shake hands in goodbye, but to Mwambu's surprise she seized his right arm with both her hands and started dragging him towards the door.

'Tell me,' she demanded, putting on a serious face, and Mwambu could not tell if she was merely play-acting. 'Tell me, is this not your house?'

'Yes, it's my house,' he said following her in. 'It's *our* house.'

'Yes, it's our house. Is your brother in Keya or here?'

'Of course he is in Keya.'

'Who looks after this house in his absence?'

'Well… um… yourself,' he stammered, and was aware of sounding stupid.

They entered the sitting room. It was a simple,

grass-thatched, mud-and-wattle, three-room house, with the sitting room in the middle and a bedroom on either side.

'That was a good answer,' she said sarcastically. 'I look after the house. I replace the grass thatch. I keep the night-dancers out. I replace the torn blanket. I keep myself warm at night. Come!'

She pushed her bedroom door open. Holding him by the hand, she led him through the door, and he let himself be conducted on the inspection tour without kicking. It was quite dark in the bedroom, however, and he felt awkward – like an intruder in the night – in the bedroom privacy. But she gave him no respite.

'Now tell me, my own husband,' she pressed on with her accusations, 'tell me how warm this bed has been for countless moons, since your brother left? How do I keep it warm? And if it's not warm, who is to blame?'

She turned sharply and faced him and threw her arms round him just above the waist-line, pressing him hard to herself.

And suddenly Mwambu took fright. *Lord God, what's this?* he asked within himself. *Please, Lord…*

'All right,' she said, breathing in heavy spasms, 'if you want to deny that it's your job to keep this bed warm, I'm going to fight you!'

Was it madness or a dream? He tried to struggle free but she held him as in a vice. Was it another of those dreams, he thought, where you run on the spot? Where you want to bolt forward but find yourself pounding on the spot, suffering, transfixed?

'Mayuba,' he said, 'please let me go.'

'No, I'm not letting you go! I'm going to fight you. I'm going to wrestle with you and tear your clothes' – *His brain somersaulted. This was like Jacob to the angel at Peniel!* – 'going to wrestle like herdsboy and herdsgirl. That will show you what you are and what I am. And then I will let you go!'

And so saying she smartly threw him on the bed upon his back and fell upon him.

'I'm going to tear your clothes!' she panted as they struggled and intertwined side by side. 'I'm going to tear your clothes… I'm going to tear the skin from your back… I'm going to claw you like a cat… I'm going to break your legs and your thighs.' Then to prove that she had thrown him in the wrestling match, she quickly lifted herself upon the elbow and sat upon him.

And so Mwambu gave up. Gave up and gave in…

When he opened his eyes at the end of an eternity, Mayuba was sitting on the edge of the bed with her feet on the floor. The moon was shining upon her face through the half-open window.

'Do you know,' she said, smiling with infinite contentment, 'that we didn't close the outside door?'

'What! Why didn't you close it?'

'Why didn't *I* close it?' she mocked. 'Is that a woman's job or a man's? Instead of minding the door you were so busy trying to kill me. Ah, you men!'

She is impossible, thought Mwambu. Really impossible. She had simply swept him off his feet, off his wits, and carried him away.

'Well,' she pronounced, 'you can now go. I'm so happy that you're not mere visitors' eggs. Oh, yes, it's true what they say, the bitter root has healing in it! Tonight I will sleep and not fret... But, oh my husband, won't you please come tomorrow about the same time and put some thatch on the roof? When it rains it leaks right on the bed and on my back.'

He got up and slunk away through the still yawning door. And as he picked his way home, a tumult of accusing voices clamoured from within and without. The moon above, the grass drooping in the way, the bushes that stood like sentries, and the very path, they all seemed to be saying, 'Mwambu, you've been wallowing in sin! We saw you weltering like a pig in pig's dung. And how you're stinking! We can smell you. You're stinking horribly. You're stinking with the flesh, the world and the devil... yes, you're stinking like the devil... like a rotten pagan...'

That same month Kuloba came riding a bicycle into the village on his way from the Second World War. He was wearing a green army uniform and a khaki cap and heavy black boots. The whole village was wild with excitement that he was back and was looking so smart. And everybody had a question for him, and he started to answer them all and continued to answer them for many days and months. What was the colour of the Germans? Did he himself kill a German? Did he see Hitler? Was there *Mutanganyi* Famine in the war also? Was it true that Jerusalem was a real town on this earth? Had he been there? Had he fought in a country of extensive hailstones or in a forest country or in a desert country...?

Mwambu came up to greet him. They struck hands together in noisy brotherly acknowledgement.

'Ah, child of my clan! How you have grown! When I left, you were only as tall as my armpit. Now we're of equal height. That's wonderful!'

*It's bad, not wonderful, Jesus! Please, God, I'm sorry. For I've now become his equal in acts of night, as tall as his armpit in darkness.*

'And so,' continued Kuloba, 'next year you must fall?'

'Oh, yes,' readily answered Mwambu. 'I was waiting for you to come back first.'

'Good! That's a good brother. I begin to swallow saliva as I eagerly look forward to eating many animals and chickens.'

An impromptu millet-brew drinking bout was organised at Masaaba's house in honour of Kuloba's safe return. Everybody drank his fill and danced to the ecstatic rhythm of the wooden back of *luhengele* to his utmost till cockcrow. The musician praised each worthy elder present by name. He sang the heroism of many warriors of old, and, moving into modern times, added Kuloba to their number.

And in appreciation of the host and hostess, he sang the goodness of their house:

'Let me sing you Masaaba
Father of this house so good
Let me sing you by your ancient name
Father of men and the mountain
And owner of a growing kraal…'

Masaaba danced with extreme satisfaction, majestically curving his arms over his head, as only the propertied ones may do, intimating his wealth in that token of cattle horns.

'And you mother of the house
Daughter of the open-handed
You provider for hungry children
O let me sing you tonight…'

Raising her right hand above her head, Nabusulwa burst into loud and long ululation of happy acknowledgement.

'And I that sing this song
Offspring of music-makers
Orphan child of Wakoneroba
See how I speak on the wire…'

Then on a lighter dismissal note, he sang the song of degrees of women to the general applause of all the men; while each woman happily believed herself to be Nasikooko, the not-too-old, not-too-young, and not-too-dead woman of experience that men prefer:

> Nasikooko is superior to the girl
> The girl is superior to the old woman
> The old woman is superior to the infant girl
> The infant girl is superior to the grave.

Mayuba danced to the very end, and Mwambu, who looked on to the very end, sadly thought what a typical Nasikooko she was. She danced with cheek and abandon and happiness. When the musician packed his instruments to go, she took Kuloba by the hand.

'My own long-awaited one,' she said, 'come, let me lead you to your own home.'

Staggering with satisfaction, Kuloba followed her obediently. Before sunrise he had passionately assumed the fatherhood of Mayuba's three-week old pregnancy.

*Chapter Twelve*

A t last the avowed year came. Kangala and Wabwire were to fall in August during the countryside season, and Mwambu in December during the school season. Kangala and Wabwire therefore declared their candidature earlier in the year. They did so during the April school holidays and so, happily for Mwambu, he was able to go about with his two friends in their regalia-gathering exercise.

As they were to dance *imbalu* of thigh-bells they needed several items. One by one they gathered them from past candidates now men: thigh-bells, head-gears made of white monkey skins, whistles, buffalo horns; and from women they gathered beads. The beads accumulated rather slowly.

'Why is it,' asked Wabwire, 'that one can't dance with one's mother's beads?'

'*Yii*, Wabwire!' answered Kangala. 'How can you dance with something from your mother's waist? Then why do people swear that they can't sleep with their mothers?'

'Oh, I was only joking,' said Wabwire, trying to minimise the import of his childish question.

'Anyway, there are always enough sisters and sisters-in-law to donate beads,' interjected Mwambu.

'And girlfriends!' added Kangala boastfully. 'Some even compete between themselves. Each thinks that if she gives the most beads, then she will be the first to benefit from one's manhood. I'm sure we shall end up with more beads than we want.'

But the truth was that Wabwire had embarrassingly few beads upon his shoulders and this reflected how few enthusiastic female well-wishers he seemed to have.

All three youths called at Kuloba's house one day to solicit some beads from Mayuba. But she told them off with characteristic insolence and joviality.

'I am reserving all my beads for my husband there in December,' she said. Mwambu felt both good and awkward. 'And why ask for beads from a happily pregnant woman?'

'Please just give me a few,' pleaded Wabwire.

'As for you,' she mocked, 'I can't give you a single one. You're wasting your time this year. You don't look serious. You better wait and dance the following one.'

But it was not that Wabwire was not in earnest. His trouble was that he had developed a slender, rather effeminately handsome body, whereas, by contrast, Kangala was stocky and rough-grained.

That evening a small supporting band gathered around Kangala and Wabwire and the two commenced their manhood dance. They danced briefly in both their homes as a start. On the following nights they danced on the village open ground. They acquired a well-known singer to sing for them. They also composed their own songs in praise of themselves and sang them. In the weeks that followed, when Mwambu was at school, Kangala and Wabwire danced till they became expert dancers. They danced high, they danced low, they danced obliquely, they danced straight, they danced all ways.

And then the decisive month of August came. Mwambu came on holiday and was happy to be with his agemates in their crucial month. The dancing became progressively more intense and the supporting crowd grew larger every successive night. Occasionally, an elder detached himself from the crowd and put his ear to the ground to listen to and assess the quality and forcefulness of the candidate's rhythmic stamping of the earth, and either nodded his head in approval or shook it in disapproval.

Kangala distinguished himself as the better dancer of the two. He was more energetic and more stylistic. And therefore it was Wabwire that the elders often enjoined to repeat a dance pattern or to stamp the ground harder. But both candidates convinced their betters that they really desired circumcision and that they would stand firm.

Day after day in open daylight they now set out to go and tell relatives far and near that this was the year of falling. They tied a colourful, dominantly red cloth on a long staff and flew it as the banner of their intended bravery, always carried high by someone in the forefront of the sauntering party.

And sauntering it really was. Walk-running, dance-running, known in the original Elgongala as '*khusanda*'. And that is why *bamakooki*, men who fall in the same year, love to call one another '*Sande imbalu yange*' – you my circumcision, you who sauntered so dearly, who dance-walked so intently alongside me for *imbalu*.

The Kangala-Wabwire party joyfully sauntered across the countryside. They crossed ridges and traversed plains. They went as far as Webuye in Kenya to tell relatives of the great dispersion of the mountain people that this was a year never to be repeated. Sauntering day and night, night and day. Through thick jungle and along wind-swept highways.

Very often the relatives slaughtered a goat, and even the very poor managed a cock or two hens, while the close aunts and uncles killed a cow or a bull. So the candidates returned home with the blessing of a cow's or goat's *chum* and of millet-yeast paste upon their brows and breasts. In Bududa, at the home of Kangala's eldest maternal uncle, a bullock was slaughtered. In Bushika, at the home of Wabwire's uncle, who had eaten all the brideswealth for Wabwire's mother, a very fat heifer, that had failed to produce a calf for many years, was slaughtered. In either case, the uncle spat unfermented millet brew on his nephew and said, 'Go and stand firm like us. We never fear *imbalu* in this clan.'

The candidates came away from Bududa and Bushika honoured and rejoicing, with bundles of the animals' carcasses, and the heifer's udder and the bullock's balls held high on two rival sticks alongside the cloth banner. In happy celebration and commitment Kangala and Wabwire alternated in composing songs and singing them. At one point they composed alternate lines of the same song:

'*Nama i bumayi*
[I am coming from my mother's clan]
>*Ho!*

*Nama i luteka*
[I am coming from bamboo land]
>*Ho!*

*Nama khu mesa*
[I am coming from mountain table]
>*Ho!*

*Nekha i mayo*
[I am descending to the plain]
>*Ho!*

*Ise nakhesa Manafwa*
[I am saluting Manafwa river]
>*Ho!*

*Ise nanina ingo*
[I am ascending towards home]
>*Ho!*

*Yino imbalu yange*
[This is my circumcision turn]
    *Ho!*

*Wo-------o*
    *Ho!*

*Wo------o*
    *Ho!'*

The rapid and pleasant wa-wa-wa-wa-wa-wa-wa of the thigh-bells intermixing with drum and rattles provided a running-walking rhythm that ate hills and valleys without rest. From time to time the buffalo-horn bearer stepped aside and importantly blew the impending news to all four corners of the wind:

'*Bv-----u!*
*Bv------u!*
*Bv------u!*
*Bv------u-u-u-u!'*

Back at home, mothers and aunts and sisters ululated loud long at the sight of the bundles of meat. Receiving the head of the bullock, Nabududa remarked, 'Yes, my son has a real uncle.' And receiving the head of the heifer, Nabushika said, 'It's a good brother who returns some of a sister's brideswealth through her son.'

Then came the day of the brewing. Three days to the day of days. Kangala and Wabwire separated and each went to his father's courtyard, picked up a water-pot, set it on his bare head, and ran down alone, all alone, to the fountain, drew water, came running with it upon his head, poured it into another pot containing millet *tsimuma* for the brew and, being now joined by a band of his supporters, danced intently round the bubbling pot.

Kangala then went down to Wabwire's home and the two danced their hardest. They danced with body and soul. Dancing into irrevocable resolution. Each assuring earth and sky that he must do it. Like father did it. Like father's father did it. Like the whole line of ancestors did it.

Suddenly a man Kangala did not know stepped out of the crowd, rubbed his hands together and gave him a very smart slap on his right temple. He winced with pain but stayed his ground and retained his composure.

'Did you think,' asked the man, 'that you too were a man five harvests ago when you shouted at me that I go and eat my mother? *Eh?* You thought I would forget. But it's the one who shits on the path that forgets; he that steps in the shit doesn't forget.'

He paused and then turned to the present matter.

'Look at me!' he called. 'Stand straight and look into my eyes. Don't twitch a muscle. I see you're crying. You're crying for it. Crying to be cut to look like your father. But *imbalu* is not laughter! *Imbalu* is a shaving knife! It's fire! It's on top of your skull! It's *pilo pilo pilo pilo pilo pilo...*'

At that very moment an older cousin of Wabwire's walked up to Wabwire and gave him two sharp slaps on either temple.

'I slap you for a good reason,' said the cousin. 'To make you strong to withstand the knife. I've noticed a certain fearfulness in you, a certain irresoluteness. But do not joke with *imbalu*, my brother! *Imbalu* is not good! *Imbalu* is agony! You have it on the courtyard, then you have it in the house. It's weeks of pain! Applying *inguwu* to the wound, that powder of the bitterest herb in the world! You put it on the wound and it smarts as if this world was buckling and cracking up! And you willingly make sure it smarts! For manhood is pain! Wilful pain…!

'Tell me,' he continued, 'are you still bent on facing the knife? If you're resolute, go on. If you have the slightest misgiving, wait for it the next time. Give me your head-gear, remove the thigh-bells and throw them down, and go into your mother's house and sit down!'

The maddening challenge was heard by both Wabwire and Kangala.

Into mother's house! No! Never! Never! Never! To return to the insults? *Ndi musinde wowo?* Am I your uncircumcised boy? Do not touch my millet-brew tube! Do not touch my gourd, my plate! I cannot share the same woman with you! Do not touch me with the filth from under your foreskin!

The first day. The second day. The third day! Cock-crow, dawn and sunrise!

The hour previously named was 'when the sun is highest in the sky'.

Each candidate was to stand on his father's courtyard, beginning with Kangala, being the son of the elder brother.

Early in the morning an ox was slaughtered in Wabwire's home, and a bull in Kangala's home. The appetiteless candidates were enjoined to eat a bellyful. There was a final blessing of millet-yeast paste and animal *chum* upon the forehead and the breast. There was pouring of libation and invocation at the family ancestral burial place. And then the administering of *ityang'i*, the toughening secret root, through the nose. Wopata administered a somewhat strong dose of it to Wabwire because of some eerie unease he had developed about him since the previous evening. 'Be strong, Wabwire my son,' he said. 'Be strong!' he repeated anxiously.

Then accompanied by the crowd, Kangala and Wabwire started running together towards the river. Namweke river. Urgent crown of mud upon the head. And in no time they were running back with the crowd excitedly following – running, flying, panting, stumbling, rising, running...

At the junction of the paths to Wopata's and Mukimba's homes, Wabwire was temporarily held back and Kangala spurred to proceed. And then the song-leader broke into 'the coaxing song,' *siwoyo*, gently and beautifully urging Kangala to fulfil that very one thing he had himself so sworn to undertake and accomplish that momentous day. The song-leader and crowd sang him forward up the hill, and he dream-floated ahead of them:

*'Mwana we batayi syalero*
[Child of the ancients today]
> *Ho-----o!*

*Syalero*
[Today]
> *Ho!*

*Syalero*
[Today]
> *Ho! Ho!*

*Bakeni bamakana bakharure*
[Visitors fantastic will appear]
> *Ho-----o!*

*Bakharure*
[Will appear]
> *Ho!*

*Bakharure*
[Will appear]
> *Ho! Ho!*

*Kumubano kumuakale kwakhulya*
[A sharpened knife is to eat you]
>*Ho-----o!*

*Kwakhulya*
[Is to eat you]
>*Ho!*

*Kwakhulya*
[Is to eat you]
>*Ho! Ho!*

*Butoto wa Mutoto wakhwimakho*
[Butoto wa Mutoto is upon you]
>*Ho-----o!*

*Wakhwimakho*
[Is upon you]
>*Ho!*

*Wakhwimakho*
[Is upon you]
>*Ho! Ho!*'

They hurried past Kangala's mother's *matooke shamba*. Through the tall grass. All the past admonitions flashing through his mind. *Imbalu* is fire... is a shaving knife... is on the courtyard... is on the head... is *pilo pilo pilo*...

Then they were dashing dementedly. Past his mother's kitchen. Rounding the main house…

'And now we abandon you! We push you to it! We push you into the courtyard! *Wo-----o!*'

He entered the enclosure of dry banana leaves. Made three leaps in the air. One! Two! Three! Planted feet firmly on the ground. Hands akimbo. Facing the mountain. And then entered Butoto wa Mutoto with the knife – and with the knife a thousand phantom voices:

> 'He has cut you the top one! …
> He has deflowered you! …
> He has started to pierce you deep! …
> He is trimming you round! …
> Leave it to him to him to him! …
> There there there there there there! …
> Sililililililililililili! …
> I!i!i!i!i!i!i!i!i!ili! …'

Hoorah! Hoorah! The three-minute eternity had ended! The eternity of the knife-blade had ended! Butoto lifted his knife high above his head to indicate that he had finished the job!

Lifted his knife high, bowed out of the enclosure, and ran away feverishly glorying in this yet another superb accomplishment of his man-maker's art!

Hoorah! Hoorah! In the house Kangala's mother heard it all.

As soon as Kangala entered the courtyard, she had dashed into the main house, crouched before the central pillar, gripped it firmly and started going through the gyrations and pangs of giving him birth. And now he was born! And now she came out of the house! Hoorah for Kangala! Ululations and other happy noises! Shouts and things in the air! Stones on the house...! For was there ever a happier mother? All the women shared in her rejoicing and came to her with mad joy.

And Kangala, the cause and object of the joy, felt the highest exultation. The most sublime relief in this world of pain. He made three final leaps in the air. One! Two! Three! Never more.

Then everybody came forward to him with homage and felicitations.

'Congratulations, Kangala, my son.'

'Yes, Father.'

'Congratulations, my brave son.'

'Yes, Mother.'

'Congratulations, Kangala. You have well finished the debt you owe to the mountain.'

'Yes. Thank you, uncle.'

'Congratulations... Congratulations... Congratulations...'

'Yes, sister... Yes, aunt... Yes, brother...'

'With this one shilling... With this small nothing from me... With this hen...'

'Thank you, brother… Thank you, sister… Thank you, aunt…'

Mwambu elbowed his way forward to offer his compliments as soon as he could and then ran off to Kangala's home.

'Congratulations, my dear friend!' he said. 'I don't have good enough words to say how splendidly you stood, and how I felt. Take this envelope as a small token from me…'

'Many, many thanks, Mwambu. Well, it's your turn next. And I'll stand by you as much as you've stood by me!'

His grandmother, his mother's mother, came dragging a live she-goat by the rope.

'You've done it, my husband!' she said adoringly. 'You've made me so happy. This animal is for you and me. Accept it from me and I'll look after it for both of us.'

'Thank you very much, my own wife,' returned Kangala with a comic smile.

And his grandfather, his father's father, came beaming with ultra-joy.

'My fellow man!' he said, shaking hands vigorously. 'My *makooki*! My fall-mate! I knew that you'd do it. Oh, you stood so firm. Absolutely firm. No winking, no twitch of muscle. That's exactly how we stand in this clan. Ever since the beginning. We stand completely still as the knife eats us. I tell you, birds have looked on your bravery and died from shock this morning. Oh, yes, birds are dying this morning.'

*Chapter Thirteen*

On hearing shouts of accomplishment from Mukimba's courtyard, an elder released Wabwire to proceed homewards. While Kangala was being cut into cleanness, Wabwire had strained and twitched like a hunting dog being held back by force from its prey. Tears rolled down his cheeks, his nostrils dilated and contracted spasmodically, and his feet were restless as if they were stepping on smouldering ash. And now the restrainer of the hunting dog let go and shouted spurring words.

The supporting crowd broke into a run. Surging up the slope. Through Wopata's coffee *shamba*. And then the song-leader started 'the coaxing song'.

The crowd from Mukimba's home came flying across by the most direct, pathless route: through bush, thorn and spear-grass. By the time Mwambu made it across, the crowd was singing the last verse of *siwoyo*, for they were nearly there:

'*Isolo isasake iyo yarura*
[See the spotted animal is approaching]
    *Ho-----o!*

*Yarura*
[Is approaching]
> *Ho!*

*Yarura*
[Is approaching]
> *Ho! Ho!'*

They rounded the millet granary, approaching the court-yard from the upper side. Then as he set his foot on the clean-swept courtyard...

Wabwire suddenly felt the inside of his head become like a sponge and swell to the bigness of a giant ant-hill.

His feet stonified into heavy clogs. All the space between his two sets of ribs went hollow... He became a spectre, alone, isolated and cast adrift in a wilderness of demons... And yet with such heavy clogs for legs he could not stop. He found himself propelled forward by numerous night-marish hands and voices...

'And now we push you to the knife! We withdraw from you! We become your enemies! We fold our hands and look on! *Wo-----o!'*

At the entrance to the enclosure of dry banana leaves there was an infinitesimal, subtle refusal of his leg muscles to proceed. But an elder's firm hands deftly guided him by the shoulders from behind through the narrow entrance. And a harsh voice said, 'No hesitating! You've eaten so many people's animals! Step boldly in!'

And in he stepped.

And in stepped after him the spotted animal: Butoto in his spotted circumciser's robe of leopard skin. Wabwire took some little while to make out his father right in front of him, his gaze wandering blankly across the faraway mountain range. Also he forgot to make the three initial leaps in the air, but nobody reminded him of it as this might have an adverse effect on him. He was keenly alive to the unbuttoning of his trousers. Then as Butoto's assistant stretched the foreskin tightly for the first cut, Wabwire momentarily lowered his eyes and caught a glimpse of the glinting knife-blade as thunderous voices chorused:

'He has cut you the first one...!' He pursed his lips and knitted his eyebrows to absorb the pain. In the split-second intermission before the next cut, his father took panic. 'Keep your eyes on me, Wabwire!' he shouted. And the crowd, knowing it was a bad start, mumbled various disapproving noises. And then came a menacing guttural bull-dog snarl...

'He has started to pierce you deep...!' It was unbearable. This was *inundula*, beginning the trimming phase on the underside with the point of the knife, a style which Butoto wa Mutoto now chose instead of using one of the two edges. This was the very apex of pain. Oh, how could he stand the serrated, jagged grating through grains of flesh...?

'*Mayi koye!*' he cried in infinite agony. 'Mother dear, I

die!' Pulling up his right leg as he so cried and twisting his whole face. This incited a pandemonium of devouring voices…

'He has destroyed his mother! Calling upon her like that! He has cried aloud! Has abominated the courtyard! Down with your leg! Fix it on the ground! Clench your teeth and relax your lower abdomen muscles!'

But from then on there was no mutual understanding, no compromise. He became a wild and mad bull, wounded and hounded by flesh-tearing goblins. At the next slight touch of the knife upon the sore wound, he howled ferociously and pushed Butoto away with both hands. And that was the end of persuasion and friendly admonitions. Four elders tried to hold him firmly on his feet but he wriggled and writhed with pain and terror.

In that event the circumciser must make a fatal cut. So Wopata gave his word for the desperate remedy.

'Hold him down on his back! I'm gone.'

He walked away with a haggard face through the displeased crowd and was followed by all his clansmen. Only the non-clansmen were left to see the rest.

In the house Nabushika broke into the saddest tears of disappointed motherhood. She relaxed her grip on the central house pillar and wept with incomparable abandon, repeatedly throwing herself on the floor and beating it with demented hands. Her fellow women drew near to her to comfort her, but she neither saw nor heard them. She was beyond consolation: for her first baby son had become terribly deformed in the process of being born…

Being a non-clansman, Mwambu stayed on through the rest of Wabwire's operation.

In thinking back on the occasion over the next many years, one simple fact always stood out clearly, engendered by the cruelty, as it appeared to him, by the cruelty of the gagging, the slapping, the taut stretching of limbs, with two heavy men bearing down on each limb to help the circumciser finish his work. The simple fact was that Mwambu wept. He wept for his friend as for a dead man, and then found himself walking away in the direction of Wabwire's clansmen.

As he passed by the women his eyes fell on Nerima, now a full-blown woman. Her eyes were red with tears, and he was so sorry that those eyes looked up into his just at that one moment, of all evil moments in the world.

'I marvel to myself,' one woman was saying, 'as to what can have caused it. Such a lovely boy to be spoilt so!'

'All through,' said another, 'he looked so well cooked for *imbalu*. He was crying for it so much all the time. I wonder if perhaps they did not give him *ityang'i* or if…'

'My fellow woman,' cut in Wabwire's eldest aunt, 'what use is *ityang'i* where some malicious man has planted his evil medicine on your courtyard?'

'Yes,' added yet another woman, 'there are such bad people in this world. They cannot bear to see beautiful children in another courtyard. How could Wabwire have feared *imbalu*? It could not be! I pity my fellow-woman, his mother.'

'Anyway,' said the aunt, 'he is better than the burnt-out gourd. Unless some monster carries him off let him be like that. He will be with us, unlike a dead child, and we shall be content to look on him.'

Wopata saw Mwambu coming towards the clansmen.

'Out of my courtyard!' he roared, mad with fury and struggling to his feet. He rushed at Mwambu with murderous hands. Mwambu quickly retraced his steps in amazement and shock, while several men instantly barricaded Wopata's way and held him.

'Out of my sight!' he bellowed. He fought to break loose but his restrainers held him firmly back. 'What! Masaaba's son to be prowling and proudly stalking about in my home! Masaaba's son! On the day of his father's witchcraft in my courtyard…!'

By this time Mwambu had negotiated his way past the women outside the main house and started running for home. He only caught fragments of Wopata's tirade as he hurried up the hill.

'… *Busungu bu----bi!* The red man's rule is so bad! It has turned men into women… Or I would have killed somebody today… Masaaba swore… Mukimba, you were there… Masaaba swore to abominate my courtyard…'

For the first time in two weeks Mwambu that evening stayed away from his two dear village-mates, with whose progress to manhood he had been so much involved. He missed the cleansing ceremony at Wopata's, the slaughtering of a black goat and the sprinkling of its blood and *chum* on Wabwire and the courtyard to take away the abomination of his having cried aloud and lain on his back. He also missed the hand-washing ceremony for both initiates.

Kangala was grieved when he learnt of Wabwire's terrible luck. Deep inside him, however, he had always suspected that Wabwire did not possess enough toughness to stand up to the ordeal of the knife. He did not believe that Masaaba had planted evil in Wabwire's path. And he was so sorry that Mwambu had been wrongly attacked as the son of his father.

Towards sunset, Butoto turned up at Mukimba's house. He had delayed so much at Wopata's house that Kangala, who was still unclean, had to eat his food with sticks. In turn Butoto now poured millet brew and water on Kangala's hands for him to wash and be forever clean. With every pouring of the millet brew and water he intoned words of blessing upon Kangala:

'Today I Butoto wa Mutoto
    have begotten you as my son
Kangala child of Mukimba
    of the Rain-makers clan
I have forever clothed you
    with the robe of manhood
And forged for you
    the cultivator's iron hoe

May you find even an elderly wife
>    though she be one-eyed
And become the father
>    of many sons and daughters.'

That night Mwambu could not sleep. The inside of his head reverberated endlessly with the day's happy and terrible noises.

On hearing how Wopata had publicly smeared him with witchcraft, Masaaba had fumed for a very long time. How could Wopata be so foolish, he asked, as to base his accusation on old and forgotten words spoken in sheer anger? Luckily for both men, however, Masaaba could not have been present at the circumcision of a *makooki's* son, or there would have been a bloody war. So Wopata's flaming wrath had fallen upon Masaaba's son.

'What a beautiful and horrible day it was, O Lord,' agonised Mwambu in the darkness of his little hut. He prayed and prayed. He prayed on his knees and then on his bed upon his back. With closed eyes and with open eyes. He prayed for calm in his innermost self and for sleep in his eyes. But the calm did not descend suddenly and he snatched a little, little sleep just before dawn, when the birds were already noisily stirring.

And then in the middle of the morning he heard a shock echo of the previous day's occurrence.

*Imbalu* was to continue on successive days, except-ing Sundays, through the remaining sub-counties of the

District. At that material mid-morning hour a hand-bell-dancing group went sauntering through the next village of Bukhontso, and the words of their song were unmistakable:

'*Wabwire elotsa i bumawe*
　　*O yaya!*
*Wabwire aterema imbalu*
　　*O yaya!*'

[Wabwire cried by his mother's clan
　　Oh dear!
Wabwire trembled before the knife
　　Oh dear!]

'Oh no!' cried Mwambu, stopping dead still on the grass outside his mother's kitchen. Or was it an ear-drum illusion? No, it was not. 'Poor Wabwire!' he aspirated. 'Poor Wabwire! How cruel and how soon!'

And at that very moment he made a critical decision: 'No *imbalu* for me in December!' Maybe after two years, he conceded, or after four years. For the time being he wanted to sort out the turbulence inside him.

## Chapter Fourteen

Back at school, Mwambu threw himself furiously into books, hoping to crowd out the memories of the vacation. As well as reading omnivorously, he went for any social and outdoor activity that was advertised.

Then one Saturday the lot fell on him to speak in a debating contest. The chairman for the evening was a top-former by the nickname of Mouthful on account of his verbosity. He launched the debate in a jovial and pompous mood:

'That in the exalted and well-considered opinion of this august assemblage of learned-heads, *Polyandry is Superior to Polygamy.* That is to say, for the edification of any weaker species here present, that being the wife of many husbands is better than being the husband of many wives.

'To my right, one after the other, are the two formidable rhetoricians of proven repute, John Busiku and Eunice Busoolo, poised, no doubt, with pregnant and impregnable proofs in appropriate support of this intriguing proposition.

'And to my left are the well-known platform orators, Abraham Mwambu and Peace Akello, lying in deadly intellectual ambush of the pretentions of the proposition, and armed, you can be sure, with dynamic syllogistic weaponry to summarily spear-head their counter-proposition.

'To each prime or primal or primary or principal speechifier, otherwise known as speaker, and to each tributary speechifier, I shall allocate an optimum of ten and seven minutes, respectively, by the rigid exactitude of my Swiss-fabricated, hand-assembled, water-tight, dust-proof, shock-protected, antimagnetic, synchronized, and automatic Roamer chronometer. Thereafter, the doubly or quadruply well-argued and well counter-argued motion shall be flung open before the general assembly for further dissection: each individual dissection not being permitted to stretch beyond the duration of three terrestrial minutes, by the rigid exactitude of the said and very same unbending and uncompromising chronometric instrument. Then the primal speakers shall each in turn, as by custom long practised, recapitulate his argument inside the confines of two exact minutes.

'Finally, it will be my pleasant and bounden duty to put the brain-challenging and heart-wracking motion to a people's popular vote. And my plea to each and every voter, which plea I shall reiterate at the opportune moment, is: please think before you vote; but if you're not going to vote, please don't think.'

The speeches were, in themselves, what Mouthful later described as very intriguing logistic and verbal acrobatics, but of no less interest were the interruptions and ejaculations from the floor.

'Shame on you!'

'Same from here!'

'Hear, hear, all you detractors!'

'Same from me!'

'A point of information, Mr Chairman. Is the Dis-honourable First Proposer in order, to bore this reputable house stiff for five entire minutes with pointless points?'

'Answer in one word!'

'Your interruption,' ruled the Chairman, 'is not a point of information but a clumsy question. Proceed, First Proposer.'

'A point of protocol, Mr Chairman! Under no circumstances is the Chairman to override reasonably framed questions from the judicious floor!'

'Hear, hear!'

'Same from everybody!'

During his delivery Mwambu kept his hands firmly stuck in his trouser pockets. Luckily for him, this posture was mistaken by the audience for a mark of self-confidence, and not of the nervousness he was trying to hide. The many eyes of all the listeners became one eye, as once upon a time at Namwombe Primary School on Parents' Day. But tonight the giant eye was not anonymous: it was Nambozo's eye. Beaming down upon him like a motorcar headlight, searching and assessing him. And it was to her that he addressed himself, and with her, for both their sakes, he pleaded before the nameless crowd:

'... Mr Chairman,' he declared towards the end of his ten trying minutes, 'in presenting our case like this, we of the Opposition have in our minds the practice of monogamy as the ideal form of marriage, and chastity as a cardinal virtue. Between polygamy and polyandry, we recommend the former as the lesser of two unnecessary evils. The idea of polyandry is, of course, unthinkable and unbearable among us Africans' – *Ah, but Mayuba, and Mayeku's wife! Who tells you I'm wife of Kuloba? I'm wife of Everybody! Wives of everybody! Mayuba and me as a secret once-for-all husband!* 'Yes, I repeat, that it is a contradiction in terms for the opposition to speak about a happy husband or a happy wife of many' – *like Mayeku's wife! Who tells you I'm wife of Mayeku?* 'There is no happiness in such a set up... For imagine a woman torn between two men...'

'*Torn!*' interjected a voice from the floor. 'She can be shared without being torn!'

'Mr Chairman,' Mwambu sallied, 'please protect me from this vicious verbal raid.'

'Granted at once,' pronounced the Chairman.

'Men who would want to *share* a woman or a wife,' Mwambu continued, *like Kuloba and myself!* 'are no better than jungle brutes!'

'Hear, hear!' yelled the audience, instantly absorbing the innuendo about their Science teacher, the wife-flogging Mr Browne nicknamed 'Brute'.

'Such a man is outwardly an urbanised but inwardly a jungle Mister Brute!'

'Wisdom! Wisdom!' roared the hall.

'And his wife is Mrs Brute!'

'Hear! Hear!'

'And his extra woman is Mistress Brute!'

'Point! Point! Wisest point! Same from here!'

'In conclusion, therefore, Mr Chairman, we of the Opposition have the honour to beg to vehemently and to most unequivocally oppose this motion. Thank you, Mr Chairman, for your indulgence. Thank you, ladies and gentlemen, for your keen attention and for voting in overwhelming support of the Opposition.'

After a balanced showdown from both sides, the motion was finally put to the vote. It was one of those rare occasions when the votes tied. Most of the abstainers were girls; and it was generally agreed afterwards that they were not sure whether they preferred to be bossed by many husbands or to be bossed by a husband of many wives. The Chairman therefore had to cast his decisive veto to tilt the balance, in favour of polyandry.

## Chapter Fifteen

On the last day of term the school truck put the mountaineers at daybreak at the farthest point on the road, where the road stopped and the steep mountain ascent started. To the left Butandiga ridge rose perpendicularly to the sky. On the other side of the ridge, said the guide, there was another much steeper path to the mountaintop through the land of Bakhama, the offspring of Mukhama, one of the grandchildren of the original Masaaba, Father of the Mountain.

At midday the small party reached the boundary of the Government Forest Reserve. This was the dividing line between the cultivated mountain slopes of human habitation and the government-protected forest of animal habitation in which men might only hunt with permission but may not settle, cultivate or fell trees.

Here in the forest reserve were gigantic trees that looked as ancient as the rocks and that grew staggeringly tall in their competition to reach the sun. Beneath the continuous overhead mat of green, the soil was soft under the foot and dark with numberless generations of myriad fallen leaves. Crossing the bamboo-uprooters' route every now and then were wild animal trails, and here and there by the wayside heaps of elephant dung from which unmasticated thorns and other remains of wood pointed outwards like spikes on some ghostly hide.

As the party steadily progressed the air became increasingly chilly.

'What you're experiencing now, ladies and gentlemen,' jovially remarked Pamba Musoke, their patron, from the rear at one point, 'is the geography of lapse fall. Needless to remind you, every 300 vertical feet we accomplish, the mountain temperature drops by one degree Fahrenheit. I dare say some people need to remember that fact for their imminent *Cantab* and to begin to get their pullovers ready.'

'We are not so cold-blooded, sir,' Nambozo shouted back from somewhere near the front of the single-file expedition.

'As a matter of fact, sir,' interjected Kalaha, President of the Mountaineering Club, 'Jane was confirmed a long time ago to be a salamander!'

'And what's a salamander?' asked Mary Nekesa, the only other girl in the party.

'Reptiles that live in fire,' volunteered Mwambu. 'Which is what Jane is saying that the two of you are by nature.'

'Nonsense!' rallied Nambozo rather coquettishly. 'I said no such thing.'

'You said no such thing,' pursued Kalaha, 'but you are the very thing.'

'Which very thing?'

'A salamander.'

'Watch your tongue, Mr President!' she warned with a smiling face. 'I'm neither a thing nor a salamander.'

'Okay, then,' conceded Kalaha, 'you're a human being, and not a salamander. So you're an ice-blooded human being?'

'Nonsense again!' she pronounced. 'I'm neither a salamander nor a pillar of ice!'

'Then, lady,' intervened Mwambu, 'you must be the average of boiling point and freezing point. You're a salamander in a fridge!'

She kicked him from behind while the others laughed uproariously. To avoid any further murderous kicks Mwambu hopped ahead and put two people between Nambozo and himself.

They traversed miles of bamboo forest in the waning sun. At the end of the bamboo zone they decided to stop for the night and to do the last, steeper leg of the climbing the following morning. The young men pitched temporary make-shift shelters and unpacked the sleeping bags while Nambozo and Nekesa played the housewives. They lit a fire and roasted some yam and bamboo shoots to supplement their packed meal. After supper they talked about an endless number of things, retold stories, warming their frontsides before the glowing log fire. Towards midnight they divided up and went to their allotted shelters under the same towering, broad-topped mahogany tree, sheathed themselves into the sleeping bags and closed their eyes in the courageous sleep of the adventurous.

But Mwambu did not quickly fall asleep, his fanciful imagination pulsating with excitement. He had this day climbed, by degrees, to within three hours of the top of the mountain. He was only a short way from his childhood dream – the top of the world's ladder to heaven. This had been the day of his ascent to the mountain of Yahweh in the land of Moriah, on which the first Abraham made an astonishing offer. And when you have brought the children of Israel out of Egypt, you shall worship me upon this mountain. Mountain of wonder. Mountain of God. God on the mountain. Man in the valleys. God on mountains... Mountain of Transfiguration... Mountain of the Sun... Masaaba's Mountain...

But the blanket of sleep had been gradually falling on him. He now turned on his side, all thoughts suspended, and he fell into peaceful slumber.

At ten o'clock in the morning the party stood upon the peak of Wagagayi, the highest of all the ridges. They took handfuls of the frozen earth and lifted it to the sky in utter ecstasy of achievement.

'Hip! Hip! Hip!' shouted Kalaha.
'Hoorah!'
'Hip! Hip!'

'Hoorah!'

'Hip! Hip!'

'Hoorah!'

'Hear ye, all ye beasts, fowl and fish;

Hear ye, all ye trees, shrubs and grasses;

Hear ye, all ye clouds, lands and waters—

That on the first day of the twelfth month

In the year of the grace of our Lord

Nineteen hundred and forty-eight

We the gallant nine together with our muse

Of Elgosec Mountaineering Club

Ascended the peak of Mount Masaaba

And engraved our signatures in the rock.'

'Hip! Hip!'

'Hoorah!'

'Hip! Hip!'

'Hoorah!'

'Hip! Hip!'

'Hoorah!'

Mwambu stood transported in the morning sun. While everybody wandered away, he remained rooted to one spot. He looked up at the vault of the sky, all round at the rim of the earth, and at the mountain sleeping below his feet like some prehistoric giant. The twin peaks of Wagagayi and Zesui vied with each other in their endeavour to pierce the sky. Between them stretched level ground for miles. This is what the dwellers on the higher slopes boastfully called

The Table. And to him a table it really was, a feast table of the Lord of the Clouds, with a fountain of the clearest water in a crater-pot to assuage his thirst.

Next, from the bottom layers of his memory, history and legend came welling up. How Mundu the first mountain man rose from a hole somewhere on this mountain. Masaaba his oldest son. Kundu his youngest son. Kundu, who, standing upon the mountain one day when the sky was unusually clear, saw a lake on the horizon in the direction of the setting sun, and yearning to go and find out the secret of the lake, journeyed many, many days and nights till he got lost, never to return. Travellers in subsequent generations telling the story of a man called Kundu, later known as Kintu, who came from the mountain of the heavens, *mu ggulu*, and alighting upon the far side of Lake Nabulolo, gradually subdued his neighbours and became the founder of a still-surviving line of heroic kings, and the father of a prodigious people, whose native language was incredibly akin to that of the far-removed Mountain of the Sun, inhabited by the great-grandchildren of Masaaba the Elder. Masaaba owner of this mountain, husband of Nabarwa, the daughter of the Kalenjin who lived on the sunrise slopes of the mountain. Nabarwa, to win whom as wife Masaaba submitted to the Kalenjin rite of circumcision and promised to pass on that rite to his offspring in perpetuity. Nabarwa and Masaaba, after his manly wound had healed, in romance coming home upon a magic cobweb string that stretched from the top of the mountain to its base. And with them upon that nuptial homecoming also came the circumciser's double-edged Kalenjin knife which…

*Ah, but that knife!* Mwambu winced involuntarily as his mind suddenly threw up the memory of the sad, pitiful cries of Wabwire on his back, cruelly fixed down by the hands of unpitying non-clansmen. Ah, that such cruel pain should be inflicted by his people, that such shame, such backward…

'Mwambu,' called Nambozo, interrupting his reverie and drawing close to him. 'I have never seen you,' she teased, 'so taken up by anything – or anybody. Isn't *she* beautiful?'

'Yes, yes!' fumbled Mwambu, sensing her playful sarcasm. 'But who tells you the mountain is of feminine gender? Is it Latin?'

'I'm not sure if it's so in Latin,' returned Nambozo half-innocently. 'Do you think it's of masculine gender then?'

Mwambu was equally caught. He must not be accused of loving the mountain as if it was a woman, or of loving it as if it was a fellow male being.

'No,' he replied, rising to the challenge, 'it's of neutral gender.'

'Okay, you win,' said Nambozo by way of setting a trap. 'You're in love with neutrality!'

It was Mwambu who was momentarily defeated. But rallying quickly, he asserted, by way of a counter-trap:

'Neutrality is the name of a certain woman without feelings.'

'The woman without feelings is Masaaba's Mountain!'

'No!' protested Mwambu. 'The woman without feelings in Nambozo!'

They were surprised at themselves. A wave of internal lightning simultaneously flashed through them both as they involuntarily held hands and he directly looked into her eyes for the first time in their more than five years of acquaintance as classmates and fellow worshippers under the Tree of God. Her eyes moistened and her lips trembled for appeasement. But quick images of Mayuba and himself on her bed and little Nerima saying, 'Hey, Nakitumba warned, "Don't touch!"' made him suddenly hold back. So he only shyly squeezed her right hand with his left, as they stood in silence side by side facing the east. And then he let go of her hand.

'We're so high up in the clouds!' he irrelevantly observed.

'Yes,' she agreed, with a trace of clear disappointment in her voice. 'Right, then, let's descend from this peak…'

'… and return to the plains,' he uneasily completed.

The rest of the party were converging around the peak from their excursions in various directions. Mwambu and Nambozo rejoined them, and the gallant nine, together with their patron and muse, started on their way down.

## Chapter Sixteen

Mwambu had sworn not to see or meet Mayuba on her own, as far as that lay in his power. But he had from time to time bumped into her and she had thrown her barely resistible challenges at him. Failing to lead him on again, she had worried herself greatly, according to a private belief of hers that a man who tumbles a woman only once and then keeps on running away from her must have found something terrible about her. And what could it have been in this case? She had often wondered, wondered and fretted.

He found himself involuntarily walking to Kuloba's house two days after the start of the Christmas vacation. It was early in the afternoon and he hoped that Kuloba would be home for lunch and still around, so as to be spared the consequences of finding Mayuba alone, maybe just with the children. But the lunch had already evidently been eaten by the time he arrived and Kuloba had gone out. Mayuba was sitting in a relaxed fashion on the verandah and talking with another woman about this inexhaustible world, which comprised the three neighbouring villages.

The other woman had been telling a story about

women's cleverness. She was Khamuka, a childhood friend of Mayuba's who was married in the next-but-one village of Ikyewa and had never had any child. It was openly said that she had eliminated her chances with extreme unselfishness in her youth and had, in the innocence of her not knowing the fact, blamed her childlessness on her evil aunts. In vain she consulted countless diviners to solicit for just one child, and in vain burnt the prescribed black chicken at riversides and road junctions to exorcise the demon of barrenness from her womb.

Mayuba saw Mwambu coming and jumped up.

'Oh, what a rare thing,' she exclaimed, 'to see you in this home, husband of mine! Today the Iteso have done a rare thing. They have consented to be circumcised...'

His blood rushed to his skin to ward off the unintentional insinuation: for the previous year he had let circumcision pass by him.

'... Oh, the Iteso have consented to be circumcised,' Mayuba repeated, pointing him to a chair. 'I shall surely tie a stone round your neck. To mark this overdue visit. I shall surely...'

Mwambu thought, *If anyone intends to cause any of these little ones to stumble, it were better for him that a stone were tied round his neck and he was cast into the sea.*

'... Sit down, rare one, and tell us, tell my friend Khamuka here and me why you've neglected me for so long. Have you no love for your own? I hate a husband who's not jealous for me...'

*Ah, Jesus, she has already started.* Yes, she had started; no preliminaries, no reserve; impudent as always and appearing to be lying or merely joking when telling the naked truth, the truth of nakedness.

'But if he's not jealous,' Khamuka broke in, 'then dance to yourself, woman, that you have such a husband. What I always tell my fellow-women,' she proceeded with self-congratulatory animation, 'is that a jealous husband is the most blind fool in the whole world!'

'What a double pity,' Mwambu observed with a grin, 'for a man to be both blind and a fool.'

'Did I never tell you about Masakwa Mukhwasi?' she asked Mayuba, taking no notice of Mwambu's interjection.

'No,' Mayuba answered. 'You must have been forgetting to do so for some selfish reason of your own.'

'Not at all. I only learnt it from a friend not such a long time ago. And you know there's no woman less selfish than me,' she ambiguously joked.

'So what happened to Masakwa Mukhwasi? Tell me.'

'Be patient, you woman, and you will hear everything. So there was this stupid husband in Kenya Colony. And his wife was from here. This man was so jealous over his pretty wife that he worried himself thin and stupid day and night. Wherever she went he was sure that all men were running after her. Very often when she went to the well to draw water, to the field to dig, or to the jungle to collect firewood, he would quietly stalk after her and watch her from behind a tree. Unfortunately for him, he never caught her out, because she didn't have a lover in that village. But she knew that he was following her whenever she went out, and that he unjustly accused her of having lovers all over the village. So she decided to show him!

'One day she told him that her brother Mukhwasi, the son of one of her uncles, was coming from the land of Mundu to visit them. But the visitor was not a brother but a former lover.

'He arrived in the afternoon. His rival killed him the biggest cock, and called him brother-in-law so many times while the two of them ate the cock and talked.'

'And what did they talk about?' asked Mayuba curiously.

'Oh, anything. Anything which was of no use. Then after the meal, when the sun was about to go to sleep, the jealous husband untied his cattle to graze a little around the house. He seated himself on an anthill near the house, and from there he continued to converse with his crafty visitor...

'Well, the following morning,' concluded Khamuka, 'the lover-visitor returned home, having eaten a big cock – and something other than chicken.'

Upon concluding her story, Khamuka looked wickedly at Mwambu and asked, 'And so how do you like the foolish and blind man?'

'I think you should ask me,' Mwambu promptly replied, 'how much I dislike your dirty untrue story.'

'Ah,' intervened Mayuba, 'that's my clean and unjealous husband speaking!'

Oh, no! Mwambu rigidly thought. She must not win again. 'Kuloba's own,' he protested firmly, 'I think it's only proper that you should call me by my right title. Which is, brother-in-law, or just Mwambu. Not husband, please! It was all right while I was still a child of…'

'While you were still what?' she snapped, putting on an offended face.

'While still a child, I said.'

'How *child* were you when you…?' He feared that she was going to blurt it all out, but she involuntarily broke off.

'Oh, yes,' she said bitingly, 'you're *only* a child. Just a small child…'

She paused for a moment and then continued, directly looking into his eyes, 'And do you know that you've never come to see us since *he* was born? And he's now such a *big* man. Almost as old as you were when mother spat into your face and you forever stopped sucking her breast!'

Again his blood rushed to his skin on being reminded of his earliest remembered thing.

'And do you know, Khamuka,' she continued, in a tone of acted innocence, 'that some wicked women in this world have been gossiping that my little Buwayirira resembles this Mwambu as if he was his *real* father?'

'Maybe as the saying goes,' laughed Khamuka, 'he passed behind you when you were pregnant. Passed behind you, in one way or the other!'

'Never! I swear that for all the time I was swelling front-wards like a woman among women, he never came near me. Did you, Mwambu?' she challenged, catching him off his guard.

'Well, um, no,' he fumbled, fidgeting on the hard *musesa* chair. 'I was busy that year with dancing *basinde* for circumcision, and with school.'

'Yes, you were *too* busy,' Mayuba mocked. 'For had you come near me that year before I got pregnant, had you come near me even for just one day, *I swear by my father-in-law*, that as you are so poisonous, you would have been the real father of Buwayirira!'

And the truth was out! Mwambu instantly interpreted her correctly with consternation. For she had seduced him *that* year! He was the father of Buwayirira! She had said it! His lips trembled and his nose perspired in remorse and defeat. For had she not delivered her baby almost exactly nine months after Kuloba's return? How could that be? He was plunged into a turmoil of self-loathing, interspersed with accusing voices reciting the scriptures. *Depart from me, oh Lord... for in me dwelleth no good thing... And sin when it hath conceived, bringeth forth death...*

'Won't you even ask to see the child?' pursued Mayuba.

'Oh, yes,' he replied dreamily. 'But you said that he was sleeping. And I actually came to visit Kuloba and yourself and not, and not...'

'Not him!' she snapped. 'I see! All right. I'll not disturb you with waking him.'

Mwambu looked away across the undulating hills in a flurry of shame and confusion. And then as he lowered his gaze – at that particular moment, of all moments in this endless world, and for no conceivable reason – his eyes fell upon an optical illusion walking into Kuloba's compound!

He sat up briskly, looked at the two women to see if they were seeing the same thing, rubbed his eyes and reopened them on the same illusion now a few paces away.

It was Nerima, his childhood girlfriend, last seen three years back, a full-grown woman. What was this, that she now appeared some six inches taller and oddly masculine in her elegant *busuuti* garment?

Mayuba said, 'We are glad to see you, visitor.'

And Nerima replied in a tenor voice striving to sound soprano! 'And I too to find you all.'

And behold, it was not Nerima but her brother Wabwire! It was Wabwire in a woman's dress!

He crouched female-fashion beside Mwambu and greeted him in the same contrived soprano. 'Peace upon you, our own.'

'Peace up-p-pon you, Wabwire,' stammered Mwambu.

'You look surprised, Mwambu,' remarked Mayuba casually. 'Didn't you know that these days this one is my fellow-woman?'

'Oh!' breathed Mwambu, unable to find more words, as if the bottom had been knocked out of him.

'Her name is no longer Wabwire; she is now called Nabwire.'

Nabwire got up from her crouching position and joined Mayuba and Khamuka where they sat on the mat.

It was too much for Mwambu! He decided that since all this must be a nightmare, there was no point in trying to behave civilly. This must be a nightmare and he in his bed doubled up and dreaming it all. So he got up and walked homewards without saying goodbye.

But the further he walked the more he started to fear that it was true and not a nightmare. The early afternoon sun did not suddenly set, as it might do in a dream. The path he was treading did not abruptly end in some yawning pit. Every detail of the path was as it had been on his outward journey. The trees still tapered upwards and the scanty clouds sailed unimportantly in the sky. He took hold of a leaf of a nearby ash tree, turned its underside up and observed its network of mid-rib and divergent veins for a lengthy moment. He knew by instinct that in dreams minute details like that never really stand out, certainly not for long, and he concluded that therefore everything he had just been through was real. That Wabwire had now become Nabwire, clad in a woman's robe.

Poor Wabwire, he ruefully mused. Poor Nabwire. What a change. He had heard of such cases before, but why Wabwire? He had heard of men declaring themselves women. There was Watoya, christened Paulo. In early manhood he had thrown off his *kanzu* and started wearing a woman's wrapper and gone about calling himself Paulina. Some people said this was a mere trick to evade paying poll-tax. But others claimed that he had truly become a woman.

But how, ruminated Mwambu, how did Wabwire end up like this? Was he born like that or did it just happen to him later, and if so, when? Before or after circumcision? If before, was that circumcision pain all in vain then? Like flogging a dead dog, or shooting a hanged man. If not, was it perhaps on the courtyard, during that cruel operation? Or did it perhaps happen while he was passing under the weeping tree? For people said that if you passed under that tree while those mischievous *ifutsani* insects were manufacturing their froth and any of it dropped on your head, that you would become impotent at once! And could it be true what people said about a he-goat restoring a man's vitality by jumping on him? Could it be that...

*Chapter Seventeen*

When they met again after the mountain trip and home, Mwambu and Nambozo were somewhat a little unsure of each other. They could not just continue from the uneasy high point where they had left off. After lunch on the first day of term Mwambu saw Nambozo leaving the dining hall a little while after him and slowed his pace to wait for her. She caught up with him and they shook hands with mutual guardedness.

'How went the holiday?' he inquired.

'Fine. How went yours?'

'Fine, too, I suppose. And how was that bamboo land of yours generally?'

'Very rainy. Not cats and dogs. It was just worms and frogs.'

'And how did you spend the days and hours?' She looked at him challengingly as if to say, Was I the substance of those days and hours?

But how could he tell her that they could all be summed up in the sad story of Nabwire? 'Oh, I didn't spend them,' joked Mwambu. 'I wasted them, and they wasted me.'

Nambozo knew he was quoting some book they were both preparing for the examinations but could not tell which.

'Is that Milton or Shakespeare?' she asked.

'Neither,' he lied, enjoying it. 'It's a melancholy of my own concoction, compounded from many nothings, and issuing from my fermenting brain.'

'Ah,' she exclaimed, 'it's Keats! It's Keats you're massacring.'

'Not at all. The man who was wasted by time is Richard II in Pomfret Castle, dreaming with wide-open eyes.'

'Anyway,' Nambozo quipped, 'that Richard is as melancholic as Keats.' Then half-seriously, she added, 'And so are you!'

'Lady, I protest!' he returned, taking up the challenge. They stopped under an acacia tree between the two class-room blocks. 'I protest against being lumped together with the tribe of Jacques and Richard and Keats and...'

'The gentleman protests too much,' she cut in, laughing and turning away. And he knew she had deliberately altered the well-known quotation.

'Let me tell you,' he continued. 'If I'm melancholic, then you're melancholitis.'

'And you're bogusinitis,' she rallied, coining a word.

'Okay! Then you're my crazinitis, my tuberculosis, my paralysis. You're my Ophelia, my Fanny Browne, my Lady Chatterley...'

'Mwambu!' she interjected. 'What an insult!' She was

in earnest. The verbal play had gone too far and they both sensed it. Her reaction was both a rebuke and an appeal to the Tree of God Christian in both of them.

'No, sister. It's not an insult.' He tried to play it off cleverly. 'Which of those ladies is an insult?'

'Lady Chatterley, of course!' she snapped. 'How can you compare me to that loose woman?' And that very moment she intuitively perceived that he had become another person since last parting from each other, after the mountain trip. There was something cruel and sad about him.

'I didn't compare you to Lady Chatterley,' he wistfully replied. 'I was comparing myself to the impotent Lord Chatterley. Or is he Sir Chatterley? I'm a cripple in love's wheelchair, and you're the kind lady pushing my wheelchair. And I'm praying to the Lord God for a miracle, for my paralysis to go. And then you won't have to push my chair.'

'And *then*,' she angrily retorted, 'you'll have no need for anybody? Is that what you're saying?' She started walking away in the direction of Lwakhakha Hostel without waiting for an answer. Whatever had come over him, she wondered. And on his part, Mwambu felt awkward about the strange tone the conversation had eventually assumed.

'See you at chapel,' she shouted back with a flat voice.

'Fine,' he uneasily replied. 'Or at supper, if I miss you at chapel.'

The Reverend James Graves had one perennial pastime well known to Mwambu and his fellows. Every year he picked and set apart one of the prettiest girls in the top form and publicly treated her as his special child. Very often she also happened to be one of the Tree of God Christians. The lucky girl thus set apart became a favourite of the Reverend Graves and his constant partner at country dance. If he passed by while she was hanging about with other students, he gave a general nod to the entire group, then, with a subtle twitch of the eyelid, beckoned her to follow him. Or he might audibly call her aside with a semblance of having some important chapel matter to tell her. If he went on home-leave that particular year, he sent her a postcard from Europe and eventually bought her a dress, a bra and chocolates. All this was with the express knowledge of Mrs Graves, who allowed it a filial, or at the very most, a platonic, status.

In her final year, Jane Nambozo was the Reverend Graves's special child. He had picked her early in the year for the shapeliness of her features, the amiableness of her character, and the alertness of her mind. She had just about stopped growing upwards and was what is known as neither too tall nor too short for a woman. She walked with a slight, electrifying spring and was the owner of a most pleasant and captivating smile. She had round, devouring eyes and that texture of black skin that people usually describe as having fallen properly upon its wearer.

These qualities had been gradually maturing in Nambozo over her years at Elgosec, at the same time as her acquaintance with Mwambu imperceptibly developed into firm friendship. The real ground of their friendship, however, was not her beauty but their heavenly common denominator, their 'Mutual Friend of the Highest Esteem, namely, Christ,' as Reverend Graves had put it once. In a meditation session under the Tree of God, the Reverend Graves had counselled all the young Christians present to regard all earthly friendships as secondary always, to admit of no friend who made demands or asked for favours that endangered one's friendship with Christ, the dearest Friend.

'You must be on your guard,' he advised, in a Sermon-on-the-Mount stance, 'against fellows who come to you saying, "I love you, I'm your best friend." What most of them really mean is that they are itching to use you. And as soon as you yield to their lies and appetites, they throw you away as unwanted leftovers from a good meal. Meantime, the Spirit of Christ flees from your heart, and in His place settles that deformed monster known as sin. You must be on your guard against pretended love, whose hidden purpose is to steer you into a merely pleasurable animal act and grieve Christ. Love is kind and patient. Love between intending marriage partners is content to bide its time till the wedding night. You must not listen to worldly men and women who come to you shouting that they love you as if you were an ice cream or a ripe mango.'

Mwambu heeded all this with intensity of purpose and prayed fervently for God's guidance in this slippery matter. He momentarily considered how tempting a ripe mango by the wayside can be to a hungry schoolboy walking home from school at the end of a hungry day. And yet every mango tree by the wayside must be in somebody's land. But there was the ripe mango, once in a long while, which falls into your path just at the precise moment when you are approaching the parent tree. You can hardly resist such a mango. It is only by God's power that you can walk on, leaving such a mango lying on the ground, he thought. And at that very instant his mind flashed back to Mayuba. She had been such a mango. And it also flashed back to the imagined moment of Wabwire passing under the tree that may have made him a woman.

*Chapter Eighteen*

Before the end of that year, Khalayi entered her own house. The winner of the tacit competition for Khalayi as wife was Murumbi, the blacksmith of the clan of Bamamomo. As soon as Khalayi started showing signs of passing from a child to a girl, the experienced eyes of old women and prospective suitors pronounced her ripe for motherhood. Murumbi's wife had given him four daughters, and he had by now convinced himself that he could only beget an heir by taking another wife, a very young wife. And so one early morning it was that he was discovered coughing upon a crossbar of Masaaba's main grain store.

'Who are you?' Masaaba demanded, a little startled as he stepped out of the house at dawn.

'A visitor of yours, old one.'

Masaaba frowned. 'A visitor of mine? What kind of visitor?'

'One that comes not to collect a debt but to ask for a blessing.'

'Blessing, young man?' Masaaba's countenance became

more austere. 'For a blessing you go to a diviner's grove, and not come to me.'

Murumbi was temporarily deflected. 'Old one,' he ventured, 'but you can bless me in a special way.'

'What special way?' Masaaba had moved to within a few paces of Murumbi.

'By allowing me,' he announced, 'to be born in your family. As your other son.'

'Spirits of the ancients!' exclaimed Masaaba, more irritated than flattered. 'What's your name and of what clan are you?'

'They call me Murumbi, son of Nyungu the blacksmith, of the clan of Bamamomo.'

'That's half a clan,' returned Masaaba teasingly, easing up a little.

'But, old one…' Murumbi started to reciprocate, but was cut short.

'Young man, are you telling me that you have seen a marriageable girl in this homestead?'

'Forgive me, old one,' returned Murumbi, 'but you know how the eye is not afraid of looking and seeing.'

'That is true,' Masaaba sourly conceded. 'But in this homestead there's not a girl but a female child.'

'It's even as you say, old one. But you know also that the infant girl is the mother of its mother. And that you're the son of your son, as I'm the father of my father.'

'Yes, yes,' agreed Masaaba uncomfortably. 'Yes, but not always.' And then he decided to end the conversation abruptly. 'Look here, Murumbi, son of Nyungu. Go back home. Go, and come back some other day, not too soon, with your elders.'

And so during that August vacation when Mwambu was at home, Khalayi left her parents' home for her own house. Murumbi's womenfolk came to fetch Khalayi on the nuptial day, insolently and provocatively singing as they danced their way into the compound how Masaaba's house was not Khalayi's:

*'Ango abene, bakhana*
*Ango abene*
*Ukenda wiwumba!*
*Ango aweffe, bakhana*
*Ango aweffe*
*Ukenda usakalala!'*

[In another's homestead, damsels
In another's homestead
You shrink as you walk!
In our own homestead, damsels
In our own homestead
You swell as you walk!]

Ululation met with ululation. Provocation with provocation. Invading women against women of the clan. Then with many gifts and many sweet words in gentler songs round the house, the invading women coaxed the women of the clan till with many sighs and many smiles Masaaba's clanswomen allowed Murumbi's clanswomen to take away beautiful, tender Khalayi. Attended by her large following of bridesmaids and choral maids, she coyly stepped out of the house of her father and mother to go and be born elsewhere, among strangers now becoming her people. Bedecked in a floral pink *busuuti* and a silken white veil, her skin perfumed with ghee and sweet-smelling herbs, away she went. A pink umbrella to match her *busuuti* was held above her head in the gentle afternoon drizzle that greeted their deliberately slow progress. Then as the party approached Murumbi's home, Khalayi's choral maids sang their provocation song for Murumbi and his first wife to hear:

*'Imbalikka yamakana*
*Kana ikhurure, yaya!*
*A--e---e E--e E---e!*
*Simakulu wa Murumbi*
*Kana akhufuluke, yaya!*
*A--e---e E--e E---e!'*

[Polygamy is such a terror
It will undo you, dear!
Senior wife of Murumbi
How she will vex you, dear!]

Shortly before sunrise two mornings later an emissary of Murumbi entered Masaaba's homestead dragging a live, fat she-goat after him. With this goat Murumbi was expressing his pleasure and thanks to Khalayi's mother and aunts for Khalayi's virgin condition up till her marriage. Through the tiny window of his hut, Mwambu saw the emissary and the goat and gave a wry smile as the meaning of the spectacle flashed through his mind, and he imagined a maiden blood stain on Khalayi's nuptial goat-skin to the delight of Murumbi.

On his way to church this Sunday morning, after Murumbi's emissary had left, Mwambu continued to feel awkward about Khalayi's going away to become a woman before he could become a man. And he admitted to himself that he must soon face up to that reality and acquit himself by one method or another.

At his childhood church, where a rickety mud-and-wattle structure with exposed ribs and a roof of rusty iron sheets had replaced the unforgettable tree of long ago, Mwambu shook hands with Kuloba after the service.

'I didn't see you enjoying yourself at Khalayi's feast, Mwambu,' Kuloba remarked jovially.

'Yes, I did,' shyly returned Mwambu. 'I ate and talked and looked on.'

'Yes, you looked on,' agreed Kuloba teasingly. And then changing his tone, he said, 'But let me talk to you about something more important, Mwambu.'

Mwambu tensed a little with apprehension as Kuloba touched his arm and led him aside. Could he have found out about Buwayirira? Oh Jesus, he thought.

'Mwambu,' Kuloba started, 'you know that you're a good Christian.'

'Ye-es,' Mwambu agreed hesitatingly, unsure if there was a tinge of mockery in Kuloba's voice. 'A Christian, yes,' he corrected himself, 'but no one is a good Christian.'

'Oh yes!' disagreed Kuloba. 'There are good and bad Christians. Good Christians do not do witchcraft, dance at night, or run after women.'

Jesus, he knows! thought Mwambu, his blood rushing to his skin.

'Don't look so put out, Mwambu,' said Kuloba with a smile. 'I'm not saying anything bad, am I? As a matter of fact, there's something I want to ask you because I know you're a good Christian.'

'What something?'

'You go to Holy Communion by now, don't you?'

'Yes, I was confirmed at school last year.'

'Good!' enthused Kuloba. 'You see,' he revealed, 'I want that little Buwayirira of ours to be baptised while still an infant.'

*Of ours!* Mwambu was stung by the insinuation.

'That will be two weeks from today,' continued Kuloba.

'So soon?'

'Yes, while you're still on vacation.' Kuloba then looked Mwambu straight in the eyes. 'Because, you see, Mwambu, I want you to give birth to Buwayirira in Jesus.'

'Oh no!' Mwambu winced as if he had knocked his foot against a stone.

'Oh, yes, Abraham,' Kuloba stressed.

'No, no, Kuloba, please.' Mwambu frantically grabbed at an excuse. 'I'm not old enough.'

'Not old enough!' Kuloba exclaimed.

'Yes, um, I mean,' fumbled Mwambu. 'I mean, yes, in church. I'm not old enough in church matters.'

'Oh, yes, you are, Mwambu,' asserted Kuloba. 'You're no longer a child. Although not yet a man by the knife...'

*Oh, my God!*

'... and you've put off that for too long.' Kuloba's tone was disapproving, accusatory. 'But that's another matter.'

*No longer a child?*

'So, in two weeks' time, Mwambu?' Kuloba pressed.

'Wh-what?' Mwambu shook himself awake. 'In two weeks' time, what?'

'The baptism, of course,' said Kuloba neutrally, 'or what else could I mean?'

'Oh, um, nothing.' Mwambu grabbed at a single meaning of Kuloba's words. And then he tried another excuse. 'But in two weeks' time I may not be here.'

'But the vacation has just started.' Kuloba sounded both perplexed and resolute.

'Yes, the vacation has just started,' Mwambu admitted, and then instantly invented a journey. 'But I was thinking of visiting a classmate of mine in Elgonton that weekend.'

'Afterwards,' suggested Kuloba. 'You can visit your friend afterwards.'

Mwambu uneasily gave in. 'All right. I'll see.'

'Good!' Kuloba was visibly delighted. 'Good, Abraham. Good, Mwambu, child of the clan.'

They started walking away together. But after only a few paces, Kuloba suddenly stopped and turned to Mwambu.

'But, Mwambu,' he said, 'I'm forgetting one important thing.'

'And what's that?' Mwambu asked with a tinge of further apprehension.

'The name. You choose a Christian name for Buwayirira.'

'Please, Kuloba!' squirmed Mwambu. 'You're asking me for too much. You choose the name yourself.'

'To choose I can,' returned Kuloba amiably, 'but you can help me not to choose a bad one.'

'There are no bad names,' Mwambu promptly replied.

'Oh, yes, there are!' protested Kuloba. 'Those which are not in the Bible.'

'And so you want a name from the Bible?'

'Yes.'

Mwambu eased up a little as they resumed walking.

'From the Old Testament,' he asked, 'or from the New Testament?'

'From the Old Testament,' came the ready answer.

'From what book?'

'From Genesis.'

'I see. From the Book of Beginnings. That's what Genesis is, isn't it? You want him to be a grandfather of men?'

'Oh, yes.'

'So how about Adam?'

'No, not Adam. It's a Moslem name.'

'Noah? The survivor of the flood, after whom came the rainbow.'

'No, not Noah, either.'

Did Kuloba want a particular name? Mwambu wondered. What name was next among the Bible elders? Abraham, of course. But he must not suggest that,' he told himself.

'What about Isaac?' he proffered. 'Or Ishmael?'

'Ishmael? Who was Ishmael?' inquired Kuloba interestedly.

'Oh, don't you know about Ishmael? He was the first son of Abraham by his concubine. Then came Isaac by his first wife. Would you like him to be Isaac?'

'No, let him be the first son,' ruled Kuloba, enthusiastically making his choice. 'Let him be Ishmael.'

'God in heaven!' exclaimed Mwambu inaudibly. 'What vengeance is this?'

'What's that you're saying?' asked Kuloba.

'Oh, nothing.' Mwambu's eyes swept across the rim of the encircling hills so green under the crisp midday August sun as if seeking assurance that all things were where they should be: the sky, the hills, the majestic mountain beyond the hills.

They came to a point where the two paths diverged, and Kuloba had to branch off to his home.

'Before I bid you stay well,' Mwambu said, mastering

his thoughts, 'let me ask you about the other godparents. You haven't told me who they are, and I was forgetting to ask.'

'Oh, that's my fault,' replied Kuloba apologetically. 'I forgot about it because we were so busy talking. The other two are myself and Buwayirira's mother.'

'What!' Mwambu exploded in exclamation. 'Mayuba and yourself?'

'Yes.' Kuloba was evidently puzzled by Mwambu's vehemence.

'Can't you ask some outsider?' Mwambu's voice was charged to the full.

'But why?' Kuloba coolly replied. 'I've certainly thought about it. Reverend Matamali says that it's permissible. Although Martha Mayuba has not been a good church-goer since our wedding, which was in the year you were born, she qualifies to give birth to children both in marriage and in Jesus Christ.'

'I see,' breathed Mwambu.

'Yes,' agreed Kuloba. 'I think it's wonderful that parents on earth can be parents of the same children in heaven. Don't you agree, Mwambu?' Kuloba sounded so gentle and sincere.

'Yes, I agree.' Mwambu abstractedly whispered.

'Good! We shall ourselves bear him in heaven.'

Mwambu nodded blankly. The two then took their separate paths at the fork and bid each other farewell. Mwambu was so relieved that the ordeal was over. But as he walked on, Kuloba's voice reverberated in his ears: That little Buwayirira of ours... No, let him be the first son. Let him be Ishmael... We shall ourselves bear him in heaven... Ourselves... Mayuba and Mwambu and Kuloba... Ourselves...

*Chapter Nineteen*

He did not stay for Buwayirira's baptism. Two days after talking with Kuloba, he left for Elgonton to stay with a schoolmate of his for the rest of the vacation. He had made up his mind, after Khalayi's marriage and his encounter with Kuloba, that during his stay in town he would go on a certain personal adventure and keep its outcome to his classmate and himself till the end of term.

The evening before Buwayirira's baptism, Kuloba decided to find a replacement for the absent Mwambu as godfather, and it turned out to be Kuloba's distant cousin, Peter Wayero, Mwambu's classmate and bully of the Namwombe years.

The baptism went on as planned, followed by festive eating and all-night drinking from a giant clay pot, around which tongues blabbed and limbs danced to the ecstasy of the drum and *sitingiti* and *luhengele* and men and women converged in the dark outside, collapsing among the banana stems and pumpkins, and Mayuba flirted with this and that man, all in general happiness together with angels and archangels and all the company of heaven over the infant citizen today admitted into the Kingdom of God.

In that outside darkness, Kuloba and Wopata and Wayero talked as they stood emptying their bladders upon the grass. They remarked on Mwambu's curious absence from the day's ceremony, which only strengthened for Kuloba the rumour that Khamuka, Mayuba's professed best friend, had intimated to him about Mayuba and Mwambu. And now the three men conferred together about staging a certain homecoming surprise for Mwambu on the day he completed school and his mother's cooking-pot pulled him back, a surprise that he would always carry as a scar in his memory. Swearing to keep their little plan secret till the day of its execution, they staggered back to the bubbling giant clay pot.

During the last three months before the decisive, terminal examinations, Mwambu's life revolved entirely around four essentials: dormitory, library, dining hall, and chapel. He would smile a quick hullo to Nambozo whenever the two ran into each other, and they would hurry to their books. That was not the time for loving or worrying thoughts. And Mwambu knew and believed that what God keeps for a poor man cannot decay. Occasionally, however, when he was restless he would seek Nambozo out for a chat, just to ease his mind. And she would willingly walk or sit with him upon the grass, happy about the change from books and endless female company. One day they went for a Sunday walk together and talked about a disconnected number of things. The setting sun gently stroked the mountain with soft, golden fingers and touched the inner self in spasms of delight. And they came back before evening chapel feeling refreshed and animated. For the rest of the evening, Mwambu was inexplicably happy, as though some unknown vacuum had been filled that day.

Weeks of books and books and books followed. Then one day towards the end of September, he felt an overpowering need to see her: to look at her, talk to her, just be in her presence for a soothing while, and then he might regain his power of concentration.

Chapel, supper and prep time and no sight of her. At 8.00 pm the class settled down to revision. He waited for another fifteen minutes but she did not turn up. He walked to the library to check there for her. But she was not there either. She must have been held up by some womanly chore in the girls' hostel, he figured. He walked in the direction of the hostel in the hope of meeting her. But he came to the end of the Library Road before sighting her. And beyond that point he could not proceed as the girls' hostel was out of bounds. So he decided to stroll about till she should appear.

But what was that trembling deep inside him? he wondered, surveying the starlit sky from east to west. The crescent moon was just sinking behind the horizon. And as he continued strolling about, sundry precious lines that he had stored away in the bottom layer of his being came welling up to the surface of memory.

Sit, Jessica, look how the floor of heaven
Is thick inlaid with patterns of bright gold...

I cannot see what flowers are at my feet,
Nor what soft incense hangs upon the boughs...

... In such a night
Did young Lorenzo swear he loved her well...

The silhouette of a spear-bearing and thickly clad night-watchman lurched into the vicinity. To be on the safe side, Mwambu coughed gently by way of announcing his presence.

'Whose shadow is that?' demanded a gruff voice.

'It's I, Mwambu.'

'And who is I Mwambu? Mwambu the long-dead ancestral warrior or a mere carrier of his name?'

'I'm Mwambu the learner in Secondary Six.'

'Aha, a learner, not a warrior! You're a false carrier of a good name.' The voice was decidedly unfriendly. The thickly clad owner of the voice was by this time beside Mwambu. He torched him in the face and down his entire height to his shoes.

'And so is Secondary Six on this road,' he demanded, 'or are you night-dancing?'

'Do night-dancers,' returned Mwambu firmly, 'walk about dressed smartly like me?'

'Smartly, did you say?' aimed the nightwatchman. Mwambu decided the man must be a recent recruit.

'Yes, smartly dressed, not smartly naked. Anyway, I'm just waiting for my sister from the girls' hostel.'

'Your sister?' The gruff voice gave an ugly chuckle.

'That's what I said. Is it funny?'

'No, it's clever. Every clever boy in your class has a sister just across in the hostel. What do you mean by a sister?'

Mwambu was amazed at the cynical temerity of the recruit. 'Daughter of one's mother or father,' he replied simply.

'Truly, truly. She that one can't touch and will never touch. That's what a sister is. And that's the type you have in the hostel, is it?'

'Are you saying that I don't have a sister?' asked Mwambu.

'No, I'm not,' replied the nightwatchman, suddenly dropping the bullying tone. 'I'm sure you have a sister somewhere in this world. Maybe many sisters. But none of them is going to come from the hostel right now. Because, as you can see, the entire hostel is in darkness. All the girls are doing prep on the other side of you.'

'Oh, I see,' muttered Mwambu, awkwardly realising that he had been talking in a losing game, and that he had not really looked at the girls' hostel all this time.

'Sleep well,' called the nightwatchman after Mwambu. The latter was retracing his steps up Library Road. 'Sleep well, smartly dressed brother of a sister.'

'In that case,' concluded Mwambu, ignoring the night-watchman's taunting goodbye, 'she must be in chapel.' How was it he had not thought of that earlier, he wondered. She must be arranging the chapel for the morning service. It must be her turn to prepare the chapel this evening.

The moon had completely set by now and the night was a shade darker as he approached the chapel. An owl on the hunt hooted its hunger among the branches of the Tree of God.

As Mwambu turned off Library Road onto the gravel chapel path, his left foot missed a step and he nearly tripped over. So he proceeded more cautiously, feeling his way with his feet, although there was no further obstacle right up to the chapel wall.

The main section of the chapel was in darkness. Only the vestry had a light burning. He could vaguely make out the low voices of the chapel wardens. On impulse, he decided to give Nambozo and her friends a pleasant surprise by entering like a ghost without knocking first. Quietly turning the knob, he gently opened the door with the slightest squeak and eased his way in. It was therefore several seconds before those inside saw with horror that they had not locked the door, and by the end of those seconds Mwambu's shocked eyes had taken in the spectre of half-naked Nambozo and the Reverend James Graves intertwined on the floor upon the Holy Table cloth for the season of Lent.

Mwambu closed the door as quietly as he had opened it.

*Chapter Twenty*

Mwambu walked away with a swollen, featherweight head, such as suddenly sprouts on a traveller's shoulders when a beast jumps into his path in the dark. He walked away without knowing where he was going, was blown past the library, past the classrooms, where others were busy with revision, past the silent dining hall, past the laboratories, past the tennis courts, circled the gymnasium, retraced his steps towards the dormitories, and seeing a light in his own dormitory, went in, mumbled something about a headache to the boys on duty, and slumped into his bed.

His brain was reeling. Reeling. Reeling as if he had spun round on his foot too fast and suddenly gone dizzy. But was it his head, he wondered, or the world that was reeling? Surely it was the world reeling, as it used to do when he was little, when he looked at the mountains and valleys from between his legs. Ah, yes, that old upside-down feeling of mountains falling into valleys and valleys falling onto mountains!

And where was God in all this daze? In the Tree of

God? Huddling with the bird which had hooted as he, Mwambu, approached the chapel. He had become a fugitive, driven out of his chief shrine by Graves. By Graves and Nambozo. Abdicated his throne, and left his regal robe behind for Graves to soil with dirty naked feet.

But that Graves. He must pay for it, he resolved. Must pay for it sooner than later. The hypocrite. The Pharisee. The masked monster. The masked monster of long ago that lured beautiful Sera into the wilderness and ate her up, and Mwambu of old had to retrieve her from the monster's stomach. Just so! Just so would he, Mwambu the younger, unmask this monster Graves, disguised in a white human shape. Yes, he, Mwambu, would drive all the white-masked monsters from the land. One day. Soon. Drive them from this mountain to the farthest lake and drown them all there. In the lake that beckoned Kundu his ancestor long, long ago. And there at the world's end, in a kingdom by the farthest lake, he would marry a virgin princess, great granddaughter of Kundu or Kintu, therefore, Princess Nakintu her name. And then he would return to the mountain country in heroic triumph, applauded by all his people for ridding the land of the monsters. Nambozo would see his maiden princess and die of shame and regret. And with Graves unmasked and drowned, he, Mwambu, and Princess Nakintu happy ever thereafter…

He had no idea as to what time it was when he fell asleep,

no idea as to how long he slept. Then in his half-sleep he dreamt that the next circumcision season had come and men went around circumcising foreigners who had mountain wives or mistresses. The first victim was Graves, who was forcibly circumcised on the altar of Elgosec chapel. Next he saw Graves's captors, handcuffed and chained together, charged with attempted manslaughter. The magistrate was wearing a white animal mask over his face.

'Accused Number One,' rang out a voice, 'what's your name and what's your job by day and night?'

And readily came the rejoinder: 'They call me Butoto son of Mutoto of the clan of Bamutoto first offspring of Nabarwa mother of the tribe and daughter of Barwa who dwelt on the sunrise slopes of this mountain and who bequeathed to Nabarwa our perpetual rite of the knife which every other harvest strikes the mountain slopes and valleys with beauty of what the eye can see and the ear can hear and I as chief man-maker of my people rising early and feverishly running to and from up and down with my glinting masculine knife making men out of boys and husbands out of youngsters and the men applaud all day long and happy lovers exclaim all night long who is it that made you this wonderful who is that made you this *wu lu lu lu lu lu lu lu...*?'

The sound of the women's ululation in his dream faded into the rhythmic strokes of the school waking drum. He stretched himself from his doubled-up position and jumped out of bed into the next day.

After their being found out, the Reverend Graves and Nambozo frantically dressed and parted in panic and remorse to their respective sleeping places. Without any tacit mutual agreement, they both stayed in bed for the next three days.

The morning following the unsavoury incident, the Reverend Graves sent a brief note to the Headmaster to say he was slightly indisposed. Mr Bentley accordingly conducted the chapel service for that morning, announced to the school that the chaplain was ill, and asked them to pray for his speedy recovery.

In the girls' hostel, the school nurse confined Nambozo to bed upon diagnosing symptoms of delirium. Her temperature was, however, quite normal, and so the nurse explained it all away as an unusual manifestation of the examinitis plague.

But what was separately gnawing away at the insides of the Reverend Graves and Nambozo was the monster scandal. On the very night of breaking what was known in the school as the Eleventh Commandment – 'Thou shalt not be found out' – the transgressors had expected instant 'Catch thief!' from the students and their being apprehended with their pants still down. But, oddly enough, there had been no such outcry, and they had sneaked away through the silent night, the Reverend Graves mumbling to himself, 'Thank goodness he didn't raise an alarm, the bastard of a peeping Tom. And how the devil did I forget to lock the bloody door?'

The painting on the vestry wall flashed through the Reverend Graves's head at his own mention of a door: Holman Hunt's rendering of Revelation 3:20, 'Behold, I stand at the Door,' in which the resurrected King Jesus with his crown of thorns, and a lamp in his hand, stands outside the door of the sinner's heart, knocking and waiting and calling to be let in, that he might light up and gladden the sinner's heart, as master and servant wondrously eat from the same vessel. Commenting on the picture to an inquisitive student once, the Reverend Graves had remarked on the absence of a handle on the door. 'Holman Hunt himself,' he had explained, 'was asked by a contemporary of his about the missing handle. And his answer was that there was only one – on the inside. In other words, Christ cannot force his way in; only the sinner can open the door, from inside.' And whenever operating in the vestry at night, the Reverend Graves had involuntarily always locked the vestry door. But tonight, of all nights, he had simply forgotten to do so. And as the meddling devil would have it, that bastard Mwambu, instead of seeing to his prep, had breezed into the vestry like some malignant ghost...

Spared for a while, throughout the following day, the Reverend Graves kept on expecting his wife to crash hysterically through the bedroom door any moment and land on his neck. But at both lunchtime and teatime Twiga returned from commandeering the school canteen looking her usual formidable self and no more.

And in Lwakhakha Hostel, Nambozo kept her eyes

permanently closed but her ears open for loud whispers from the corners of the dormitory, but she heard none by the end of the first day, and none by the end of the second. On the third day she feebly beckoned her friend Nekesa to her bed.

'How is eating books going?' she asked.

'Fine,' replied Nekesa. 'How is examinitis treating you?'

'Not fine. How is everybody?'

'As usual.'

'How is Mwambu?'

'Okay, I'm sure. Devouring words and figures.'

'Have you seen him today?'

'No, not today.'

'Have you seen him these three days?'

'Yes. Yesterday. Why do you ask?'

'Does he know I'm unwell?'

'But, of course. The whole school knows.'

'What!' Nambozo looked wildly about her. 'What! The *whole* school?'

'What's the matter?' asked Nekesa. 'Don't sit up, you're feeling very weak. If only you knew what nonsense you've been saying in your sleep, you'd…'

'Oh, no!' cried Nambozo, springing up and sitting stiffly upright in her bed. 'What have I been saying? Tell me!'

'Nothing. Indistinct noises.'

'No! Tell me, what did you hear me say?'

'Nothing, Jane. Believe me, nothing. I could only make out "Chapel", "Love" and "God." Nothing more.'

'Nothing more? Just chapel, love and God? How curious. And how is it the *whole* school knows about it, Mary?'

'But what's wrong with the whole school knowing about it? You've just been suffering from malaria, not VD or...'

'Ma---ry!' screamed Nambozo. She gripped Nekesa's hand. 'Why the whole school? Who told them?'

'Goodness me, Jane, what's wrong with you? I told a few friends, that's all. But you know how words travel. Maybe the nurse also told some people. You should know that you're not an unimportant woman.'

'Woman?' She looked wildly about her again. 'Who says I'm a woman?'

'Well, what *are* you?' asked Nekesa simply, hiding her fright. 'Are we girls any longer? I'm not! Are you?'

'Ye---s, I'm a *girl!*' stressed Nambozo. 'I'm not yet out of school!'

Nekesa was by now convinced that her friend was truly sick. 'You've gone back on wanting to be called a girl?'

'Yes!'

'A Cantab woman still a mere girl?'

'Yes, I say!'

'That's like when the Reverend Graves once said...'

'Mary!' she shouted, flinging the pillow at Nekesa. And then Nekesa knew that there was something terribly wrong with Nambozo.

'Jane—' Nekesa started to say.

'Like the Reverend Graves?' moaned Nambozo. 'Like

the Reverend Graves? Mary, you're bad. What did you tell people that I'm suffering from?'

'Examinitis, of course.'

'And what did the nurse tell them?'

'She never said anything to anybody. She only told me that you had fever without a temperature.'

'So it was you who told the whole school! Mary, you're a rumour-monger!'

'Not I. I was only joking about telling the whole school.'

'Then who told them? Was it Mwambu?' she spurted.

'What! Why Mwambu?' Nekesa was at a loss. How on earth could Mwambu have anything to say about her illness?

'Well, what has he said about me?' she demanded.

'About you? Mwambu? Why, nothing! Nothing, my dear.'

'Are you sure?' She held Nekesa's hand imploringly. 'Are you sure?'

'Very sure. Did he say or do something cruel to you?'

'No. He has said nothing. He has said or done nothing. Nothing cruel. Nothing…'

Nambozo lay back in her bed, closed her eyes and breathed calmly as though a balm had been thrown upon her troubled spirit. Nekesa noted this with wonder and relief and tip-toed away.

The following day Nambozo was quite recovered, and the nurse was easily persuaded to let her take a walk to her classroom.

During evening prayer the same day, as Nambozo entered the chapel she noticed the Reverend Graves in a back pew with other members of staff. He was bowing in silence before the start of the service, not kneeling upright but had rather slumped into himself in a praying arc that momentarily blurred before Nambozo's eyes.

*Chapter Twenty-One*

Through the rest of the term Mwambu contemplated the best way to announce the spectacle in chapel. He was not going to leave Elgosec quietly, he decided, after what he had seen with his own eyes. No!

He had surprised himself the following day that he had not raised the alarm. Then the whole school would have come running and the profane copulators would have been apprehended with their cloaks and masks cast aside. Yes, that's what he should have done, he rued, and yet his tongue had just stuck to the roof of his mouth, and he had speechlessly walked away.

What was the matter with him, he wondered, that he had never done anything tough, except perhaps thrown a brick at Wayero long ago at N.A.C Namwombe Primary School, never done anything manly…

He suddenly checked himself at the thought of manliness, catching himself out. He stepped aside to let a classmate, who was following him, go ahead towards the classroom. Then as he reached the verandah of the classroom block, his mind flitted to the *Macbeth* they were revising that morning, and he grinned to himself as on a number of occasions before, as Macbeth's words to his pestering wife crossed his mind:

I dare do all that becomes a man
Who dares more is none

He smiled sardonically as he once more puzzled out Macbeth's ambiguous words: I dare do anything that is proper for a man? That is right for a man? He that does more than that is not a man? Not a single man dares more than me? If anyone dares more than me then he is not a man? He is... What? Mwambu had often wondered. And today as he went through the classroom door, he fleetingly thought: To dare more than a man and be less – was it daring to be Wabwire and end up as Nabwire?

One day before the official end of the term, Mwambu sat down to break his silence over the Reverend Graves and Nambozo:

Manafwa House,
Elgon Secondary School,
On 21st Anniversary, Founder's Day.

To: Mr Arthur Bentley,
Headmaster, Elgon Secondary School,
Private Bag,
Elgonton.

Dear Sir,

### A Vision of Hell in the Chapel

This is to inform you of a vision of hell that I, Mwambu, saw in the former House of God at Elgosec on All Saints' Day, that is, 1st November this year.

Being led by an inner prompting, I entered the chapel at about 8.30 pm, during prep time. Softly turning the handle of the vestry door, I pushed my way in – and behold! *The truth struck and dazed my eyes. That the Devil had thrown God out of Heaven!* For there on the vestry floor before my very eyes was a couple of naked demons, male and female, upon the Holy Table cloth for the season of Lent, lost in erotic abomination! While I was rubbing my shocked eyes to see better, the vision vanished – and look! – there sprung up upon that very spot the human forms of Graves and Nambozo! These two are my witnesses to the truth.

Your Past Christian Student,

   Kiboole Mwambu son of Masaaba

Copy to: School Notice Board.

He dropped the letter in the staff mail box and posted up the school copy on the notice board while everyone was having lunch. Then walking to his dormitory and picking up his bag, he left Elgosec and chapel and the Tree of God and the God of Graves for good.

By the time news of his vision of hell had circulated round the school, which was within fifteen minutes after the end of lunch, Mwambu was nowhere to be seen.

Nambozo ran into Lwakhakha Hostel shouting hysterically, and, falling on her bed, buried her face into her pillow. And Mary Nekesa, as before, came to her with soothing explanations.

'That Mwambu!' she swore in a rage of confusion, and anxious to side with the vulnerable Nambozo. 'All this time he must have been hiding such a sick brain! To imagine all that rot and write it, post it up, and then take to his heels! What a dangerous liar! What a coward! What a milksop!'

And the Reverend James Graves gravely came play-acting into the school. All the students looked at him with a dubious grin as he entered the Staff Room for the emergency meeting hastily called by Mr Bentley.

During the meeting the Reverend remarkably kept his countenance as a sign of his innocence. Everybody at the staff meeting agreed that Mwambu was always something of a lone dreamer, possessed of a demonic imagination.

And it was, in conclusion, resolved that his examination results would be withheld till he came back to Elgosec and was made to confess his rotten imagination upon his knees.

Meanwhile, the Reverend Graves was advised to proceed overseas on home leave, to renew his mind and spirit.

He that so often had quoted those favourite lines of scripture, about the magical renewal of the faithful!

> They that wait upon the Lord shall renew their strength,
> They shall mount up with wings as eagles,
> They shall run and not be weary,
> They shall walk and not faint!

He had indeed more than once preached on the text and informed the school that according to an antique Jewish belief, when an eagle was beginning to grow too old to mate with its kind, it dived into a far-away mystical lake, from whence it returned to its base a rejuvenated, potent eagle!

## Chapter Twenty-Two

A t Elgosec Corner, Mwambu hailed a rickety lorry. Into it he climbed and headed for Namwombe and home. He had sent word to his father and mother to say that he would be home the day before the official end of term. The day of his return to the world of his childhood was therefore known to the entire neighbourhood through the women's exchange of news at the fountain as they drew water at sundown as ever and filled their pots and pans, talking and laughing over them and parting at the rim of the trough of the fountain.

The lorry put him at a road junction seven hills from his home. He reckoned that he would reach his home well before the sun reached its own. He walked at a steady, adult pace, periodically shifting his bag from his masculine arm to his feminine one and occasionally stopping to rest for a while in the shade of a wayside tree. At the top of the third hill, the highest of the seven, he was thrilled as he looked towards N.A.C. Namwombe Primary School with its early recollections, and beyond that at the towering distant mountain range bathed in the radiant late afternoon sunshine.

'Father,' he found himself repeating his infant question, 'Father, shall we reach the top of the mountain? Have you ever touched heaven? No?'

No, Masaaba, his father, had never climbed the mountain. Mwambu grinned at the thought. No, his father had not been to the top of the mountain, never been to N.A.C Namwombe, to Elgosec, to the Tree of God, to chapel, on All Saints' Day that year, had not gazed at naked Graves and... and...

He forcibly pulled his mind away from the disturbing chapel sight and continued his journey down the hill.

Three hills later, with one more hill to go, he was going past the homestead of Mandu, father of Wayero, his old-time classmate, when his attention was drawn to a small gathering in a temporary grass shelter erected in the middle of Mandu's front yard.

'Is that you, Mwambu?' asked a curious and loud voice from the gathering. Wayero of long ago stepped out from the shelter, and then Mwambu knew from whom the hidden voice had come. 'Come and greet people, Mwambu,' continued Wayero, acting friendly and familiar.

Mwambu hesitated for a while and then walked over to meet Wayero. On the ground opposite the door to the main house were two bundles of dry banana leaves, each beautifully strapped from one end to the other by broad bands of banana fibre, and Mwambu knew the two formed the mattress of a circumcision initiate.

Wayero read Mwambu's mind and said, 'Today is my

young brother's day of burning his boyhood mattress. He was circumcised during the harvest season.'

Mwambu's eyes uneasily wandered from the mattress to the drinkers around a pot of millet brew in the grass shelter, and to his surprise, he recognised among them his cousin Kuloba and Wopata, father of Nabwire that used to be Wabwire.

Wayero brought a chair from the main house for Mwambu and placed it near the entrance to the shelter.

'Sit down, Mwambu,' he said, excitedly rubbing his hands. 'We haven't met since the very beginning of the world! Sit down, and welcome home.'

'Yes, welcome home, Mwambu,' added Wopata's voice from the shelter.

'Well completed the books,' complimented Kuloba from the far side of the pot.

'Welcome and well done!' chorused everybody in the shelter.

Then all of a sudden a youth came running from the direction of the kitchen with a flaming grass torch, and, as suddenly, everyone in the shelter came hurrying out and stood round the mattress of dry banana leaves. Mwambu involuntarily stood up to see for himself what was amiss. Touching one end of the mattress with the flaming torch and looking at Mandu his father, the youth intoned,

'Today do I set a firebrand
To you, mattress of dry banana leaves.'

And touching the other end of the mattress with the flame, he continued,

'Today do I set on fire
My past of uncircumcision,
Today burn to ashes my pubic skin.'

Then he was up and sprinting away through the crowd that stepped back to clear the way for him. And as he fled he recited words that gripped Mwambu with awe and novelty:

'See how from home I gleefully run,
By opposite route to return at sunset
To life cleansed by knife and fire.
See how I emerge like butterfly from chrysalis
See how I moult like serpent from ancient skin.'

The emergent man disappeared round a bend down the hill. All eyes then switched back to the flaming mattress, as everyone stood in silence for an intense, timeless while. The silence was abruptly broken by a youth with a woman's wrapper around his loins. Circumcised only two weeks back, upon belated return from long sojourn in a distant district, he now abruptly tapped his long, decorated initiate's walking stick on the ground and yelled:

'Wo-----we!
Go tell Mwambu son of Masaaba

Who has overslept before the knife

To come and drink unfermented beer.'

Mwambu instantly panicked while the entire gathering burst into derisive, calculated laughter.

'Go tell him where?' asked Wayero. 'This is the very Mwambu,' he added, pointing at Mwambu.

'Yes, this is the very Mwambu!' shouted the crowd in well-rehearsed unison.

'Mwambu!' Wopata menacingly called and stepped forward. 'Why have you never paid your debt to the mountain?'

'Yes, why?' chorused everybody.

'How many more granaries do you first want to devour?' asked Wayero bitingly.

'Answer that!' demanded Kuloba, only two persons away, latent animosity in his voice.

'Let me te-te-tell you,' stammered Mwambu.

'Tell us what?' Wopata gruffly cut in. 'Do not tell us, but pay your debt. Your debt to the mountain here and now!'

'Yes, here and now!' concurred the crowd.

'Let me tell you that I have…'

'Don't tell us anything!' roared the crowd. 'Not words but payment!' Four men seized both Mwambu's hands and held them behind him, while the fifth man burst into the finale circumcision song, and from the rest readily came the response:

*'Umusinde sikonera uyo wema'*
[See the overdue candidate standing]

    *'Ho------o!'*

    *'Wema'*

[Standing]

    *'Ho!'*

    *'Wema'*

[Standing]

    *'Ho! Ho!'*


From behind the grass shelter Butoto wa Mutoto the circumciser came dashing towards Mwambu with a drawn knife.

'You people!' screamed Mwambu, frantic with confusion. 'I want to tell you that I...' But his mouth was slammed by a heavy hand.

'No talking on ritual courtyard!'

Two appointees quickly undid Mwambu's trouser belt. Then they fumbled with his buttons one by one, while sundry admonitions and commands were flung at him.

'As by choice you refused it, by force accept the knife... We today circumcise you... Make you a man before you reach home... To go tell Masaaba your father how you picked manhood on the road... Down with those trousers and cut him clean!'

And down came the trousers – at once revealing an utter surprise to all the onlookers amid a riot of exclamations and questions.

'What! How! When and where were you circumcised? By whom and why? Tell us at once, you cheat! Tell us…'

Those who had held his hands behind him released them and came to the front to see for themselves.

Regaining a little composure, Mwambu pulled up his trousers and started buttoning them.

'When were you circumcised, Mwambu?' demanded Kuloba disappointedly.

'Three months ago,' replied Mwambu, looking Kuloba straight in the face. 'On the day Buwayirira was baptised.'

'What!' shouted Kuloba, insulted by the coincidence. 'Did you have to do it on that day?'

'Yes.'

'Why?'

'Because that's the day I happened to see the doctor!'

'The doctor?' sneered Wayero. 'Were you circumcised in hospital?'

'Just as you say,' replied Mwambu, as from the crowd came a storm of further questions.

'Was the doctor a man?'

'Or an *Etesot?*'

'Or a woman?'

'Or a eunuch?'

Mwambu made no reply, momentarily unsure how to answer the insults, and this only aggravated the annoyance of the chief planners.

'Circumcise him again!' shouted Wopata in an enraged voice. 'Circumcise him properly!'

Everyone burst into laughter at the ludicrous proposition.

'No, no, no,' protested Mandu with a wry smile. 'He has been circumcised enough as he is. Who ever heard of anyone circumcised a second time? Who of us ever bled twice from the knife?'

'You're right,' concurred another elder. 'One is done only once. Otherwise how would one ever swear by the knife? That it's as true as I cannot be circumcised a third time?'

Another burst of laughter rang from the crowd. And then the atmosphere cleared a little. The main actors in the pre-arranged drama with an unforeseen ending started walking back to the brewing pot in the grass shelter.

'All right, Mwambu!' shouted Wayero, feeling outsmarted and duped. 'All right, mistah. Tuck in your shirt like a good little schoolboy, hide your tail and go. But never you be the first,' he superiorly ruled, 'to open your mouth in the council of real men.'

'Never you be the first,' added Wopata, 'to put your tube in a pot of beer.'

'Never you risk castration,' pronounced Kuloba, 'by being caught with the wife of a proper man!'

'And now – go,' growled Wayero.

'Pick up your enlightened bag,' mocked Kuloba, 'and go tell Masaaba your father and my father's brother, that you're not a man.'

'Go tell him,' Wopata complemented, 'that you're half a man!'

Mwambu dizzily took up his bag and walked away from the derisive crowd. He was feeling both distressed and delighted: distressed at being so crudely set upon; and delighted at the unexpected disclosure of his recent quiet hospital circumcision. But as he plodded up the hill against the setting sun, a turmoil of emotions fought within him. A turmoil of emotions and memories and voices of home and Namwombe and Elgosec were echoing inside him: *You a man! To go harassing me for my breast as if it is yours! And now don't cry any more... Manfully to fight under Christ's banner... I dare do all that becomes a man... Who dares more is none... And now go tell Masaaba that you're half a man...*

*A Glossary of East African Words and Phrases*

| | |
|---|---|
| *aterere mukhwasi* | 'Shall I tell you, my brother-in-law?' |
| *bamakooki* | See *makooki*. |
| *basinde* | The uncircumcised. |
| *bazungu* | White men. *Muzungu* is the singular form. |
| *busuuti* | Elaborate dress, now the women's national dress in Uganda. (Also known as *Gomesi*.) |
| *Etesot* | A male adult of the *Iteso* tribe. The *Iteso* do not have the custom of 'the knife'. |
| *fainolo* | End-of-term settling of old scores amongst schoolchildren. (A play on the word 'final'.) |
| *fotifoti* | English, as it comically sounds to native ears. |
| *ifutsani* | The dripping sap of 'weeping' trees. |
| *imbalu* | Circumcision. |
| *induli* | An edible fruit, of a golden colour when ripe. Proverbially 'the sweetest and loveliest' of fruits. |

| | |
|---|---|
| *inguwu* | A herb whose leaves are dried and crushed into the smarting medicinal powder made for the treating of the circumcision wound. |
| *inundula* | A circumcision style whereby the trimming begins on the underside in such a way as to maximise the pain. |
| *kanzu* | A long-sleeved garment of Arabian origin, now the national dress for men in Uganda. |
| *khutyekula* | To dance with light, zestful steps. *Tyekule* is a contracted version of this. |
| *kumutoto* | A large evergreen tree. |
| *litungu* | A lyre with seven strings. |
| *luhengele* | Musical instrument consisting of an oval hollowed-out wooden vessel and two sticks. |
| *lufufu* | A mythical herb used in bringing the dead to life. |
| *makooki* | A man circumcised in the same year as oneself. *Bamakooki* is the plural of this word. |
| *matooke* | Plantain. |
| *matsima ni kwoku!* | 'It's true, I swear with my hand up!' |
| *mpioko* | A newcomer in a school. |
| *mu ggulu* | In heaven. |
| *musesa* | A simple wooden chair. |

| | |
|---|---|
| *mutanganyi* | A sour mixture of soya and maize flour which was rationed during the Second World War famine. |
| *muzungu* | See *bazungu*. |
| *mwatu ejakait, empaako? yaawo* | 'My dear sir, what is your pet name?' |
| *nguuli* | An unpurified form of Ugandan gin. |
| *shamba* | Field. |
| *sitingiti* | A musical instrument with two strings. |
| *suka* | A wrapper, worn mainly by women. |
| *tafadhali unisaidie* | 'Please help me.' |
| *tsimima* | Roasted millet dough with which millet brew is made. |
| *tyekule* | See *khutyekula*. |
| *waragi* | A refined form of *nguuli* (gin). |

## The Meaning of Several Names in the Novel

| | |
|---|---|
| *Bakhama* | A small semi-tribe on Mount Elgon. |
| *Bamamomo* | Iron-ore Clan. |
| *Bumutoto* | The clan where circumcision is said to have started. *Bumutoto* candidates are the first to be circumcised, on the first day of January. |
| *Kalenjin* | An extensive ethnic group that stretches from Uganda into Kenya. |
| *Kundu* | Thing, object. Name given to a child born after many dead siblings. |
| *Masaaba* | Name of the ancestor of *Bamasaaba*, who are also known as *Bagisu*. |
| *Mayuba* | The cheeky one. |
| *Mukimba* | Rain maker. |
| *Mundu* | Man. Father of Masaaba, the ancestor. Equivalent to Adam. |
| *Murumbi* | Blacksmith. |
| *Mwambu* | The legendary hero of Lumasaaba folklore. |
| *Sera* | The legendary sister of Mwambu. |

*About the Author*

TIMOTHY WANGUSA is a novelist, poet, and professor born in 1942 in Bugisu, eastern Uganda.

He studied English at Makerere University and began working there in 1969, becoming the first Ugandan Professor of Literature in 1981. He has since served as Minister of Education in the Ugandan government and as a Member of Parliament.

His debut novel *Upon This Mountain* was published in 1989 and is still studied in secondary schools in Uganda. Its sequel, *Betwixt Mountain and Wilderness,* was released in 2015. Wangusa has also been included in numerous poetry anthologies. His poetry collections include *A Pattern of Dust: Selected Poems 1965-1990* (1994) and *Africa's New Brood* (2006).